''That little boy's sufferin'....''

A grimace of pain crossed eighty-four-year-old Thom T. Taggart's face. ''He needs a mama and a daddy full-time.''

Seventy-one-year-old John Hayslip Randall IV nodded. ''Agreed. Unfortunately, his parents barely seem able to share the same room without starting the Civil War all over again.''

The two men slumped back in their chairs, united in heartache. After a while, Thom T. looked up. ''Too bad we can't just lock 'em in a room like a couple of wildcats and let the fur fly till they work it out,'' he growled.

''Desperate times call for desperate measures—but how do we get those grandchildren of ours to cooperate?''

''Cooperate, hell! We're talking blackmail!''

A silence; then John leaned forward. ''It might work,'' he said slowly.

''Gotta work! 'Course, there'd be fireworks....''

Ruth Jean Dale says that Texans are, quite simply, the greatest—especially Texan men! In fact, she was so taken with the Texan hero of *Fireworks!*, Jesse James Taggart, that she decided to write three more stories featuring the "Taggarts of Texas." Look for these upcoming Harlequin titles: *The Red-Blooded Yankee!*—who's a Texan by blood, if not by birth—Harlequin Temptation #413, October 1992; *Showdown!*, Harlequin Romance #3242, January 1993; and *Legend!*, Harlequin Historical #168, April 1993.

Books by Ruth Jean Dale

HARLEQUIN ROMANCE
3097—SOCIETY PAGE

HARLEQUIN TEMPTATION
244—EXTRA! EXTRA!
286—TOGETHER AGAIN
315—ONE MORE CHANCE
380—A MILLION REASONS WHY

FIREWORKS!
Ruth Jean Dale

Harlequin Books

TORONTO • NEW YORK • LONDON
AMSTERDAM • PARIS • SYDNEY • HAMBURG
STOCKHOLM • ATHENS • TOKYO • MILAN
MADRID • WARSAW • BUDAPEST • AUCKLAND

For my favorite Texans—
my daughters Valerie and Sarah,
my sister, Margaret,
my niece Kellie
and my friend Fran, the terror of Wichita Falls.
Yawl the greatest!

ISBN 0-373-03205-6

Harlequin Romance first edition July 1992

FIREWORKS!

PROLOGUE

St. Louis, Missouri,
the first week of June

THE TWO OLD MEN eyed each other warily across the marble table in the private dining room of Ye Olde St. Louis Hostelry and Purveyor of Fine Foods and Spirits. This meeting between eighty-four-year-old Thom T. Taggart of the Rocking T Ranch of Texas and John Hayslip Randall IV, seventy-one, of the Boston banking Randalls, was due entirely to circumstances beyond their control. These men would never be friends, but they did accord each other a certain grudging respect.

"Taggart."

"Randall."

They shook hands briefly.

"So how is young Jesse James?" John inquired with a slight curl of his patrician lip. He drew out an antique side chair, fastidiously flicked an imaginary speck of dust from the seat and sat down.

Thom T. plunked his expensive Stetson hat onto the table and shoved a hand through his wild white hair. His dark eyes flashed. "You just cain't let that go, can you? You been told time and again the boy was named for his *uncle* Jesse and his *great-great-grandpa* James."

The old cattleman dropped into a chair, glowering. "But to answer your question, my grandson is right as rainwater. Or he would be if that girl a'yours would—"

"I'll brook no criticism of my granddaughter," John interrupted fiercely. "Meg's doing the best she can. It's not easy, raising a child alone—" He broke off as if realizing he'd confessed his granddaughter was less than perfect. He cleared his throat and patted the vest of his dark three-piece suit.

"She's raisin' my great-grandson alone by her own choice," Thom T. pointed out. "And she's doin' a danged poor job of it."

Randall flushed darkly. "The boy may be . . . somewhat undisciplined, but he's only seven years old."

Thom T. snorted. "I ain't talkin' discipline. I like spirit—raisin' a little hell ain't a bad thing at any age. But that boy . . ." The old man sighed and shook his head. "It pains me to say this about my own flesh and blood, but that boy is danged near a *sissy.*"

"You go too far, sir!" John banged one fist on the marble table, jarring Thom T. "That boy is the apple of my eye. I won't tolerate such talk—from anybody!"

"I ain't *anybody!* All you gotta do is look at the boy to know he's more Taggart than Randall. And when it comes to lovin', why, I love that boy more than—" Thom T. broke off as if searching for a superlative strong enough to convey the depth of his devotion. "I love that boy more than the whole danged state of Texas!"

John's mouth dropped open and his eyes widened. "In that case," he said, recovering, "I am willing to concede that you have come to this summit meeting with the best interests of the boy at heart. As have I.''

Thom T. gave an emphatic nod. "You can bet yore boots on it, Johnny. I wouldn't mind seein' the boy's daddy a mite better off, neither. He's been between hay and grass way too long, far as that girl a'yours is concerned.''

"I beg your pardon—between hay and grass?"

Thom T.'s expression plainly said "dude." "Neither one thing nor the other. He ain't married and he ain't single. That girl a'yours left him—what, four, five year ago?"

John nodded. "I never approved of the marriage, you know that . . .''

Thom T.'s snort expressed accord.

John pursed his lips. ". . . but I have to agree that a wife's place is with her husband.''

"Well, now, in all fairness to that girl a'yours, it ain't always easy to figure out where a rodeo cowboy's gonna be, let alone be with him." Thom T. looked as if he didn't want John to appear the more magnanimous. "A'course, Jesse is thirty-two and I think he'd have give up rodeoing by now if he had anything better to come home to.''

"Meggie never cared for his profession."

"Not many women do—married women, that is. The single ones like it fine.''

The two men exchanged knowing glances. The silence stretched out between them.

Finally John said cautiously, "I suppose it's too late for them to resurrect the marriage.''

"Prob'ly," Thom T. agreed. "I don't hold with divorce, but I reckon sometimes it's the only answer.''

"Divorce." John's distaste was clear. "There hasn't been a divorce in the Randall family for generations—perhaps ever."

"That a fact? And you folks comin' over on the *Mayflower* and all that," Thom T. said with barbed innocence.

John turned a fierce gaze on his companion. "Divorce would be better for Randy than this . . . this half family. His parents are neither truly married nor truly divorced, and neither one of them seems willing to confront the situation. A boy needs a father—"

"Ain't that what I been sayin'?" Thom T. blazed.

"A *father,* not necessarily the man who *fathered* him. If Jess and Meg can't provide the boy with a stable family situation, then Meg needs to move on and find someone who can!"

Thom T. drew a quick harsh breath. He looked ready to lash out; then a grimace of pain crossed his face. "The boy's sufferin'," he admitted in a gravelly voice. "He needs a mama and a daddy full-time."

"Agreed. Unfortunately, his parents seem barely able to share the same room without starting the Civil War all over again."

The two old men slumped back in their chairs, united in heartache. After a while, Thom T. looked up.

"Too bad we can't just lock 'em in a room like a couple of wildcats and let the fur fly till they work it out," he growled.

The air hung heavy with revelation. Slowly John straightened. "Perhaps you've inadvertently hit on the answer—if you could get that grandson of yours to cooperate, that is."

"Cooperate, hell! We're talkin' blackmail!"

"Coercion, if you please. Blackmail is such an *ugly* word."

"Call it anything you danged well please. I can handle Jesse, but there's no way in the world you could get that girl a'yours to do it."

"I could if I threatened to cut off her trust fund."

"You'd do that if'n she balks?"

"That and more. Not that I'll be put to the test. You have no such bargaining chip to get young Jesse James to participate."

Thom T. leaned forward confidently. "I got no financial hold on him, that's true enough. Him and Boone was both left well-fixed when their folks died—filthy oil money, but it spends just like the real thing." His grin grew crafty. "Got me a ace in the hole, though."

"Which is? Out with it, man!"

Thom T. took his time, obviously enjoying the other man's impatience. "I can threaten to sell the Rocking T."

John looked disappointed. "You think that will be enough?"

"Hell, yes! Jesse purely dotes on that ranch, and he'll get it when I cash in my chips—which I ain't plannin' to do in the foreseeable future. Ain't another soul in the family cares about the place, includin' his brother."

Another silence; then John leaned forward. "It might work," he said slowly.

"Gotta work. We're just about at the end of our rope, far's them two's concerned." Thom T. cocked his head at a challenging angle. "'Course, there'd be fireworks."

John shrugged off the warning. "Desperate times call for desperate measures. Where—?"

"Where they spent their honeymoon, where else? It's a'way back there in the Texas Hill Country, miles from anything 'cept'n that one little bitty ol' town."

"As I recall, they never went there again."

"Yep. Place should be just a'brimmin' with good memories." Thom T. winked. "That little gal a'yours ain't much of a wife but she's a looker!"

John started to retort, then apparently thought better of it. "Perhaps this would be a good time to order lunch while we work out details," he suggested with a stiff formality. "I'd like to fly back to Boston tonight."

"Good idea. You wanna ring for that matter-dee?"

John did so. "They serve excellent steaks here," he said in his pompous manner.

"Yeah, well, I get enough steak back home in Texas. I'm gonna have what I always have when I come to Sa'nt Louie," Thom T. allowed.

"And that is?"

The old cattleman chortled. "This town's only got one arch, but all I can think about when I look at it is a hamburger!"

San Felipe, California,
the second week of June

JESSE JAMES TAGGART held fast to the top rung of the chute, glaring down at the wildly plunging horse they called Widowmaker. Around him swirled the dust and heat and noise of the rodeo, but his thoughts were far away.

The woman's got nerve, I'll grant her that. Blaming me because she can't handle Randy. Almost unconsciously Jesse patted the letter burning a hole in the pocket of his plaid shirt. *She babies the boy,* he thought with grim certainty. *What that kid needs is a firm hand and some good old-fashioned seat-of-the-pants discipline.*

What that kid needs is his father.

"Good luck, sugar!"

Distracted, Jesse spared a quick glance over his shoulder. The redheaded barrel-racer who'd been pursuing him so relentlessly stood there, smiling. Jesse gave a noncommittal grunt and tried not to stare at the woman's ample cleavage.

She drew a deep breath, which didn't help his resolve a whole bunch.

"Honey," she drawled, "you couldn't melt me and pour me on that bronco." She winked, clearly suggesting that he might melt her for other purposes.

Jesse swallowed hard and yanked his attention back to the job at hand. This was Meg's fault, too, he fumed. It was easier to scratch your ear with your elbow than to convince predatory females that the wedding ring he wore still meant anything when—

"Watch it, J.J.!"

The shouted warning came just as Widowmaker reared, flinging back his big ugly head. For a split second his crazed glance connected with Jesse's. The horse's wild eyes promised hard times ahead for any cowboy dumb enough to crawl on board.

"Man, better you than me!" One of the cowboys fighting to control the bronc raised a sweaty face to Jesse. "This ol' hoss has got blood in his eye!"

Jesse grabbed the suitcase-type handle attached to a leather strap rigged just behind the plunging animal's shoulders. Easing down into the chute, he wrapped powerful legs around the infuriated horse. He glanced at the man leaning over to help. "I'm gettin' too old for this foolishness," Jesse growled.

"Hell of a time to get religion," the cowboy shot back with a cheeky grin.

Yeah, well, timing's never been my strong suit. It's also a hell of a time to admit Meg can't handle my boy. Kid's got spirit. All he needs is a firm but loving hand, not some snooty private school where they'll make a sissy out of him—

"—J. J. Taggart of San Antone, Texas, a former world champion, comin' out of chute number five on Widowmaker. That hoss made his name the old-fashioned way, folks—he earned it!"

Yeah, Jesse decided, *it's time I stepped in and made my presence known. He's my son, too, and—*

The gate banged open. Widowmaker charged out, practically breathing fire. Jesse, caught napping atop the roughest bareback bucker in the string, lasted about two hops. He hit the dirt of the rodeo arena hard and lay there, stunned. Trying to catch his breath, he slowly acknowledged every ache and pain in his thirty-two-year-old body.

Damn, I really am gettin' too old for this life, he thought as his eyes began to focus. He blinked, trying to concentrate on the figure perched like a vulture atop the chutes.

Now, what would Thom T. Taggart, better known to Jesse as Grandpa, be doing in California? The old codger hated airplanes worse than carpetbaggers, and flew only under duress. Jesse rolled over onto his

knees and shook his head, trying to clear it. He was
going to need his wits about him and soon.

The rodeo clown loped over and leaned down. "You
okay, J.J.?"

Jesse nodded groggily. With a quick pat on the
shoulder, the clown turned away to take a pratfall,
delighting the grandstand. Jesse ventured another look
at the chutes.

It was Thom T., all right, gesturing "come here"
with one forefinger. Jesse didn't need to see the dia-
bolical expression on his grandfather's face to know
he was in trouble.

*Meanwhile, across the continental
United States in Boston, Massachusetts*

MARGARET RANDALL TAGGART—Meg—tried to keep
her thoughts from wandering as Felicity Holliwell
droned on about the upcoming benefit for a new wing
at the children's hospital. Meg had volunteered her
grandfather's Boston town house for the committee
meeting, and a half-dozen public-spirited women were
in attendance.

It was a generous gesture she now regretted. Not
that this wasn't a worthy cause; it was. But at the moment, Meg had other things on her mind.

Like the telephone call last week from Jesse. *Criticize me, will he! The man's got more nerve than a
Boston cabdriver.*

Felicity caught Meg's eye and Meg gave the woman
a blank smile while her thoughts tumbled on. *It's easy
to sit clear across the country and criticize. So Randy's not perfect—what child is? But he's not a sissy,
no matter what Jesse thinks. He's not!*

"Then that meets with your approval, Meg?"

At Felicity's question, Meg jerked her wandering attention back to the business at hand. She had no idea what was going on, but she automatically nodded as if she did. Felicity was trustworthy, after all, unlike *some* people Meg could name.

Felicity beamed. "I knew we could count on you to head the publicity committee," she said warmly. "Geoffrey will be so pleased. He's promised to work very closely with you."

Geoffrey! Meg stifled a groan. The head of public relations for the hospital was the last person she wanted to deal with. The man had made advances— yes, advances! At first she'd thought she was imagining things, but when he got her alone last week in the linen closet on the fourth floor of the hospital . . . No, it wasn't her imagination.

And me a married woman! she thought indignantly. *What does he think my wedding ring is, window dressing?*

"Now we need a volunteer to chair the decorating committee," Felicity announced. "Meg did such a brilliant job with decorations last year that she'll be a hard act to follow—"

Randy darted into the room, skidding to a stop when he spotted the women. His seven-year-old face was set in petulant lines Meg knew well. She spoke quickly, trying to head off catastrophe. "Come say hello to my guests, darling, and then you must run off and play for a few minutes longer."

Randy thrust out his lower lip. "Yeah, hi," he muttered ungraciously, not even looking at those to whom he presumably spoke. "I'm tired of waiting, Mom. I gotta talk to you *now*."

"As soon as my meeting is over, honey. Why don't you go out to the kitchen and tell Tess I said it's okay for you to have a snack?" *And we don't need a replay of that little scene at breakfast,* she added silently. It would be too humiliating in front of these women.

Felicity cleared her throat, a disapproving sound. "Now, as I was saying—"

"No! I don't want a dumb old snack from dumb old Tess! I wanna talk to you *now!*" Randy's freckled face turned beet red below his pale straight fringe of hair. His gray eyes, so like his father's, flashed.

Suffering agonies of embarrassment, Meg turned toward the watchful committee members. She might have her difficulties with her son in private, but he had never been allowed to make a spectacle of himself in public—never! "If you'll excuse me," she said calmly, "I'm afraid I'll have to deal with this little crisis first. Please, go on with the meeting."

She crossed to Randy and put her hand on his shoulder in a grip that meant business. "Come into Grandfather's study, dear, so we can talk."

"I changed my mind. I don't wanna talk anymore." He shrugged away from her hand. "Just tell me, do I get a new bicycle or not?"

That topic had been exhausted several times already; he knew very well the answer was no. Perhaps he thought that she'd agree now to avoid embarrassment. She struggled to keep her face impassive as she took a step toward him. He retreated, staying just out of her reach. "This is neither the time nor the place—"

"I hate that dumb old bike I got for my birthday. It's for babies!"

"Then don't act like a baby," she said sharply. *Spoiled, Jesse said. Too easy on the boy, Jesse said.* Well, she'd show Jesse! She fixed Randy with a narrow-eyed gaze. "Young man, I want you to march out of here this minute and wait for me in your grandfather's study."

For one wonderful moment, Randy hesitated, and she thought her new approach was going to work.

It didn't.

"No! I hate you!" The boy clenched his hands into fists and his voice rose. "You're mean! You don't love me!"

Meg rocked back on her heels, a feeling of helplessness washing over her—so much for Jesse and his bright ideas about firm discipline. Randy had never been so openly defiant.

She reached for the boy again, but he ducked and whirled away. Off balance, he stumbled, plowing into a marble pedestal supporting a glass display case. Slowly it tottered, the case sliding toward the edge....

The display case containing her grandfather's treasured Ming Dynasty vase, wobbled...trembled... toppled from its perch. The horrid sound of shattering porcelain and glass mingled with the shocked exclamations of the women. At that precise moment, John Hayslip Randall IV appeared in the doorway.

"Ladies," he said formally, tipping his head in greeting. His glance settled on the destruction at his feet and his expression hardened.

"Grandfather!" Meg licked dry lips. "I...I didn't know you were back from your trip. We seem to have had a little...accident here. Randy..."

She glanced around, confused; Randy was gone, slipping away through the other door.

Her grandfather gave her a tight-lipped smile, crooking one forefinger at her in an unmistakable summons only she could see.

"Ladies," he said again, and walked out of the room. Humiliated almost beyond endurance, Meg followed with her head held high.

CHAPTER ONE

HELL'S BELLS, TEXAS, proclaimed the sign on the edge of town. 2,506 NICE FOLKS AND A FEW OLD GROUCHES. Meg slowed the rental car to a crawl. The first time she'd seen that corny sign she'd been a bride, enchanted by her new husband and her new life.

Boy, was *that* long ago and far away, she thought as she pulled in beside a combination gas station and convenience store at one end of the short main street. Farther down she could see the Hell's Bells Low Life Saloon, and the Lone Star Texasburger Drive Inn. Gritting her teeth against memories, she climbed out of the car and walked quickly to the small store.

Now that she was so close to her destination, she suddenly found herself desperately thirsty. With trembling hands, she opened the cooler and pulled out a soft drink—she didn't know what kind and didn't care. She carried it to the counter.

A freckle-faced woman of perhaps forty-five hurried up from the back of the store, her smile wide and genuine. "Howdy, yawl," she greeted. "What else can I do you for?"

It took Meg a moment to recognize the Texas version of the Southern, "Hello, you-all." She smiled. "You wouldn't have any out-of-town newspapers? I meant to pick up the *Boston Globe* at the airport but..."

But I got rattled at being back in Texas and forgot.

"'Fraid not," the woman said, as cheerful as if she'd been the bearer of good news. Punching numbers into the cash register, she surreptitiously looked Meg up and down, taking in the cream-colored slacks and linen blazer. "Flew in to San Antone, did you?"

"Yes." Meg counted out change.

"You lookin' for the Hell-on-the-Handbasket Dude Ranch?"

Meg popped the top on her can of pop. She supposed she did look like a dude. "I didn't know there was such a place," she said, procrastinating for all she was worth.

"Oh, sure. Joe Bob Brooks opened it up a while back. Doin' right good, from what I hear. It's on Handbasket Creek—used to be the Box B."

"I know where the Brooks ranch is." Meg regretted the stiffness that had appeared in her voice, but mention of Joe Bob caused her already low spirits to sag even more. She lifted her can in a farewell salute.

"Oh." The woman frowned and bit her lip, her curiosity almost palpable. "I'm Laurel Anderson. If you're visiting—wait a minute! I know you." She actually hopped up and down in excitement. "You're J.J.'s wife."

Meg swallowed hard. She hadn't been linked publicly with Jesse in years and it was a little...scary. "Uhhh, how...?"

"Old Thom T. come in a couple days ago to open the cabin. Stocked up with food, even brought in some horses—guess J.J. wouldn't come otherwise." Laurel laughed and followed Meg through the door into the ninety-degree heat. "I bet you and your handsome

husband are lookin' forward to a second honeymoon.'' She winked. ''My, that's romantic!''

Meg tried for a natural smile and felt herself fall
short. She had counted on anonymity, obviously no
longer possible.

Laurel halted beneath the awning, just out of the
glaring sunlight. ''I guess I'll see yawl at the big Fourth
of July wingding?''

''Maybe.'' Meg gave the other woman a vague wave
and a wooden smile. Walking quickly to her car, she
climbed in and drew a deep breath.

She hadn't wanted to come here in the first place,
and now that she was getting close to her destination,
she wanted it even less. So what was holding her here?

She could turn around and drive back to San Antonio and catch the first plane home. Her grandfather wouldn't cut off her trust fund . . . would he?

That issue was in doubt, but other issues were more
clear-cut. Such as Randy—she was at her wit's end
trying to cope with him. Love wasn't always enough;
she needed help. The twenty-four-hour-a-day responsibility had worn her down, yet she was afraid to relinquish additional authority to the boy's father.

Jesse . . . She pressed her lips together in an unhappy line. She'd spoken to him on the telephone but
she hadn't seen him in more than two years. Had he
changed? Did he still possess the power to enchant? Or
would she be no more attracted to him than she was
to . . . to Geoffrey, half PR man and half octopus?

Somehow she doubted it. She started the engine,
hesitated, then pulled out onto the two-lane street.
This time she wouldn't run.

THE TAGGART CABIN lay in a bend of Handbasket Creek, seven miles southwest of town. To get there, Meg had to drive right past a sign hanging over a gated entrance that read HELL-ON-THE-HANDBASKET GUEST RANCH, JOE BOB BROOKS, PROP.

The last time she'd seen Joe Bob, he'd been on the rodeo circuit with Jesse—his best friend, in fact. Jesse'd spent a lot of time hauling Joe Bob out of one scrape or another, and trying to smooth over the repercussions of the man's abominable practical jokes.

Meg hadn't disliked Joe Bob—at first. He disliked her, though, showing his feelings in dozens of subtle ways that seemed to go right over Jesse's head. When she mentioned any of this to her husband, he'd just shrug and tell her she was imagining things.

Remembering upset her all over again. Which was good—she needed to keep past grievances in mind when she faced Jesse, she reminded herself as she drove into the clearing in front of the Taggart vacation cabin. Unless he'd changed drastically, he wouldn't be an easy man to resist. She'd have to be constantly on her guard.

She saw him at once, stripped to the waist and wrestling a corral pole upright in a freshly dug hole. He shifted the pole, positioning it, and the muscles of his smooth brown back rippled with power. Meg shivered.

Jesse James Taggart stood six foot one in his stocking feet, which always made Meg feel even more petite than her own five four. In cowboy boots he was taller yet, although this particular pair was old and battered and rundown at the heel.

His jeans, faded and soft from countless washings, glossed over his lean hips and muscular legs like ma-

ple syrup over hotcakes—Meg licked her lips and
forced herself to look away. Turning off the engine,
she reminded herself firmly that thoughts like these
could get little girls in trouble—and big girls, too. She
must keep her mind on the business at hand.

Her grandfather had made his wishes—no, his re-
quirements—perfectly clear.

"You and Jesse are too stubborn to get back together and too stubborn to get a divorce," John Randall had said with uncharacteristic bluntness. "You're
locked in a battle of wills and you're hurting your son.
You and Jesse James Taggart *will* come to some
agreement before you return to Boston—and that
means deciding once and for all whether this cocka-
mamy marriage is on or off."

You're hurting your son. Guilt engulfed her like an
ugly cloud. Was she a bad mother? Doubt spawned by
remorse had made her bow to her grandfather's
blackmail. She wouldn't have given in to all the threats
in the world, not for all the tea in China. But for
Randy, she'd do anything.

A fight had been brewing with Jesse, anyway, about
the Pickerell Day School for Personal Potential. It'd
probably take months of unpleasantness to get him to
agree to that one. But the school *was* for the child's
own good and she'd make Jesse see that. Whatever
faults he might have, she believed he loved Randy and
wanted what was best for the boy.

Which was just about the only good point she was
willing to concede to him. She sighed. If only Jesse
wasn't such a self-sufficient loner. If only Jesse wasn't
so misguided.

If only Jesse wasn't so gorgeous, she amended as he
stood upright, away from the corral post, and dusted

his hands across his thighs. Only then did he turn toward her, as if he'd been in no hurry to renew old acquaintances.

The sight of him took her breath away, just exactly the way it had the first time she saw him eight years ago. Then, he was out of his element on a ski slope in Aspen. Now he was in his element, and she was in a lot of trouble.

He slipped his battered Stetson off a post and slapped it on his head. Grabbing his chambray shirt off the top rail of the corral, he walked toward her with that loose-limbed, rangy gait she remembered so well. He didn't smile, nor did she.

She just stood beside the rental car like a mouse waiting for the cat to make up its mind whether to attack or play.

He stopped ten feet away. Cocking his head to one side, he narrowed his gray eyes. Absently he lifted the sweat-stained hat and pushed damp strands of dark hair away from his broad forehead with one forearm before replacing the hat. Then he shrugged into his shirt, his attention on her face never wavering.

A shame to cover that body, Meg thought, watching him do so. His chest was smooth and heavy with muscle, his belly washboard-rippled. She knew the texture of his skin, the density of his—

"You need a haircut," she said abruptly, turning away because she could no longer bear the sight of him. The memories of him—

"You don't."

His voice, a voice she hadn't heard in more than two years except distorted by the telephone, sent prickles up her spine. She'd always found that low raspy quality enormously sexy—*Stop this,* she ordered herself. *You will not let yourself be drawn into that trap.*

"What's that supposed to mean?" she tossed over her shoulder.

He followed her to the trunk of the rented Honda. "You cut your hair. I liked it long." His tone accused her of a breach of faith.

Guiltily she touched the short silky curls, caught herself doing it and pulled her hand down. "I cut it more than a year ago. Everybody *else* likes it this way."

He reached past her to raise the car's trunk. "But it was so pretty before, all long and silky and—"

He stopped short, but it was too late. Their glances met and she knew he, too, was remembering the way he had spread her hair over the pillow like a silken sham.

His face hardened. "At least you didn't change the color."

"Why would I change the color?" she flared, reaching for a small leather case. "I'm perfectly satisfied with brown hair, even if you have a penchant for blondes."

"Damn it, I don't have a..." He straightened, his jaw tight. His eyes became hooded and his voice dropped to a malevolent purr. "Maybe blondes have a penchant for me."

Meg held herself still for a mental count of five. "This comes as no surprise to me," she said gently, then picked up a case and turned toward the cabin.

Unfortunately, she was trembling so badly that discretion seemed the better part of valor. Rounding the back of the car, she set the case on the ground and drew a deep breath.

After a moment she said in a strangled voice, "The cabin looks the same."

"Yep," he said from behind her. "The cabin's the same. *We're* different."

She couldn't argue with that, so she concentrated her attention on the thirty-by-forty-foot log structure. Nestled in a grove of oak trees, its rectangular shape was further softened by Handbasket Creek, meandering past not thirty-five-feet from the back door.

A stone chimney indicated the fireplace within, the only source of heat. A porch wrapped around one end and halfway down the front.

Meg knew that Jesse's great-great-great-grandfather had started construction on the cabin back in the fifties—the eighteen-fifties. Not long afterward, family ranching interests had moved a couple of hundred miles north to the Rocking T. But the Taggarts had kept the cabin on the Handbasket, tangible reminder of their birthright.

It had begun with only one bedroom, but succeeding generations had added to the simple structure. When Meg arrived eight years ago for her honeymoon, it had three bedrooms, plus a kitchen, dining area and living room.

Her honeymoon—she wouldn't think about that, not now, not ever. Grabbing the leather case, she stalked up the two steps onto the porch and pushed through the doorway.

Once inside, she stopped so short that Jesse stepped on her heels. Over his murmured apology, she spoke with crisp decision. "I'll take the front bedroom."

"I'm in there. You can have the big bedroom."

"The master bedroom?" She raised one eyebrow. "You take it. You are the master, after all."

He refused the bait. "I got here first so I got first choice and I chose the front bedroom. You can take the big bedroom."

Meg turned left, down the short hall. "In that case, I'll take the back bedroom."

"That room's no bigger than a good-sized closet," he pointed out, following with the remaining bags. "Besides—"

"I *said* I'll take the back bedroom." She paused at the closed door and shot him a challenging glance.

"But—"

"My mind is made up, Jesse. I *want* this bedroom and I'll *have* this bedroom and that's that!" Actually, she amended silently, it wasn't so much she wanted this bedroom, she simply *didn't* want the master bedroom.

Where she'd spent her honeymoon.

"Far be it from me to stand between the lady and what she wants." Jesse's faint smile looked sardonic around the edges.

He reached past her for the doorknob, his forearm brushing her shoulder. She flinched, catching herself almost at once, hoping he hadn't noticed.

He pushed the door wide and his smile broadened. It was that same infectious grin that had so attracted her— She pulled up her rambling thoughts and turned away.

He was right; she wouldn't be moving in here.

The bed was gone. In its place were stacked cans of paint and piles of brushes and sheets of wallboard and building supplies she couldn't even name.

"Oh, for heaven's sake!"

"Big bedroom? Your choices are limited. It's that or...sharing."

She felt her cheeks warm. "Come on, Jesse, trade with me," she wheedled.

"Not a chance."

"But I don't want—"

Something blazed in his clear gray eyes. "You think I do? Look, you're not the only one who's fighting memories."

She drew herself up with dignity. "Who said anything about—?"

"Okay, deny it," he interrupted impatiently. "Deny it till the cows come home—what do I care. I didn't want to come here in the first place." He shook his head in evident disgust. "Those two old goats have really outdone themselves this time."

"Don't you call my grandfather an old goat!" Meg marched across the hall and into the "big" bedroom—all of twelve-by-fourteen feet. The bed, an elegant hand-carved four-poster, stood against the far wall. She tossed her bag on the quilt coverlet.

Jesse slammed the two suitcases down on the braided rag rug beside the wooden rocking chair. "Don't tell me you're here of your own free will."

"Of course not." To give herself something to do, something besides look at him, she unzipped the bag and started removing cosmetics.

"So how'd John get you to come?" He lowered himself carefully into the antique rocking chair, as if he expected it to collapse. It didn't.

"Threatened to cut off my trust fund. How about you? What did Thom T. hold over your head?"

"Said he'd sell the Rocking T and buy an old folks' home in Florida."

She laughed at his glum expression. "You didn't believe that!"

"Not until Boone put in his two cents' worth. He's been after Thom T. to sell for a coon's age. Thinks the old guy's too old to be playin' cowboy—those were his exact words."

"Your brother's got a point," Meg observed reasonably.

That earned her a frosty glance. "My brother is in London and hasn't got the first idea what's goin' on back here. He should mind his own business, and I told him so."

"Before or after you knuckled under to save the Rocking T?"

A sheepish grin curved his lips. "After." He lifted the hat from his head and, with a flick of his wrist, sent it sailing toward the bed. It caught on a footpost and whipped around in a circle, as neatly pegged as if...

As if he'd done it before—and he had.

Meg clenched her fists. "Please," she said in a voice that caught somewhere deep in her chest. "If this is my room, I'd like some privacy."

For a moment she thought he'd refuse. Then he sprang from the rocking chair and crossed to the doorway in two long strides. Pausing, he looked back at her from beneath lowered brows.

"I lied," he said in a flat challenging voice. "I didn't come because of the Rocking T. I came because of Randy. You think I'd put myself through this for anything short of love?"

HE'D COME for the same reason she had. After he'd left the room, she stared at the closed door and tried to ignore the sinking sensation in the pit of her stomach. What, after all, had she expected?

Moving numbly, she forced herself to unpack, to arrange her cosmetics in the bathroom, to hang her clothing in the small cedar-lined closet. Every move, every decision challenged her self-discipline, but she persevered.

Her thoughts were more difficult to control. For years she'd managed to brush off contemplation of the mess they'd made of their marriage. Now it was painfully obvious to her that as long as she was here in this place, she'd be able to think of little else.

The truth she'd long avoided demanded recognition—the truth that when she and Jesse married, they'd had nothing whatsoever in common but love.

Walking across the room, she reached up without thinking to pluck the Stetson hat from the bedpost. She looked down at the sweat-stained white felt with the leather headband pressed against her breast. Her heart leapt. Touching Jesse's hat was almost like touching Jesse.

Filled with panic, she flung the tangible reminder of him across the room, as far away as she could get it. It skidded across the top of the small dresser placed against the wall and slid off the opposite end. The resulting clatter told her it had taken something else with it.

She knelt and picked up the hat. Beneath it lay a picture frame, face down in a scattering of broken glass. Carefully she shook the frame free of shards and turned it over.

Her wedding picture—she remembered that day as if it were yesterday. The camera had caught them staring into each other's eyes with a kind of wonder.

They'd known each other for two weeks—she tried to console herself with the knowledge that it was a miracle they'd lasted as long as they had.

She didn't believe she'd ever managed to become a central part of his life. She had clung to her Eastern ways and he to his Western ways, and neither had tried hard enough to blend the two into something workable.

He had never really needed her. She hadn't wanted to admit that, but events finally forced her to face the truth. When she left, he hadn't come after her. It was as simple as that. As painful as that.

Minutes ticked past as she knelt there on the floor, trying to make sense of the predicament in which she found herself.

And trying to figure out why he still wore his wedding ring.

AT SIX O'CLOCK, Jesse knocked on her door. "Supper's ready," he called.

She listened to the sound of his retreating footsteps, then put aside the novel she'd been reading—more accurately, the novel she'd been holding. With unwilling steps, she left the room to join him.

Jesse stood behind the open counter that separated the kitchen area from the living-dining room, a big pitcher in his hands and two glasses before him. Meg walked to the wooden dining table and pulled out a chair.

"So what's on the menu?" she inquired, sitting down. "Pheasant under glass? Chicken à la king? Bologna sandwiches?"

Jesse carried the two glasses to the table and set one before her. "Nope. We're having *real* food." He turned back toward the counter and the two bowls waiting there.

"I'm almost afraid to look." Meg picked up her glass and took a hearty swallow. "Arrgh!" She curled her lip and slammed down the glass. "This tea is sweetened!"

"So? That's how I like it." He set a bowl in front of her and stuck a fork upright in its contents. "Beans and wieners," he announced with satisfaction. "Enjoy."

She should have known. She really should have known. Jesse had never been much of a cook. *Be fair,* she reminded herself. *Neither was I.* The difference was that she knew her limitations. He didn't. Instead of cooking what he liked, he liked what he could cook.

Or open or thaw or microwave, or eat cold or raw. Anything you could spread on a cracker or stuff between two slices of bread or roll up in a tortilla was okay with him.

This dish fulfilled a number of these prerequisites. All he had to do was open a can of beans, hack up a package of wieners and dump the two together. Sometimes he heated it; sometimes, like now, he didn't bother.

He ate with gusto, finally glancing up. He frowned. "Look, when you do the cooking you can pick the menu," he said. He put his fork down as if he'd lost his appetite.

Meg felt a flicker of guilt for ruining his meal, although heaven knew why she should. She plucked her own fork from the bowl and considered the two beans speared by the tines. "I suppose that's fair," she conceded. "You caught me by surprise, that's all. I haven't tasted this since—"

She broke off and began to eat. They both knew "since when"—since the last time he'd thrust them upon her. "Not bad," she said after a moment.

"Could you learn to like it?"

"No."

Their glances met with smiles that refused to be stifled. The tension eased.

Meg carried her sweetened tea to the sink and poured it down the drain, refilling her glass with water. "I think I could learn to tolerate your food peculiarities a little better now, at least," she conceded, sitting back down at the table. "To prove my good faith, I'll fix breakfast tomorrow."

Jesse leaned back in his chair, his surprise only partially feigned, it seemed to her.

"I can't wait. Thom T. stocked three kinds of cold cereal so we won't starve."

That crack might have made her angry but it didn't. She wrinkled her nose to show her disdain and picked up her fork again, finding herself ravenously hungry all of a sudden. "So what are we going to find to do around here to keep from going crazy?" she asked between bites.

"Sure as hell not the same thing we found to do the other time we were here," Jesse shot back.

Meg felt her cheeks flame. Every word she said, every word he said, seemed loaded with double meaning. Blast those two old men for their conniving! Appetite gone again, she pushed her bowl aside. "Am I going to have to watch every single word I say to you?" she demanded.

"Think you could?" He reached for her bowl and her hand tightened on the rim. His eyes asked a question; slowly, she uncurled her fingers and let him draw her bowl away.

"No, and I don't think I want to," she said, watching him use her fork to eat from her bowl. "It was really rotten of Grandfather and Thom T. to do this to us."

"Yep, but they don't care whether we like it or not. From their point of view, they're justified."

"You're defending them?"

"Hell, no! But I understand why they did it. They're worried about Randy. *I'm* worried about Randy. *You're* worried about Randy. The kid's turning into a—"

"Don't say it! Don't you dare call him a sissy! He's just a baby."

"I don't have to say it—you said it for me. And he's not a baby. He's a kid who's tied to his mama's apron strings."

She half rose from the table, both palms planted flat as she leaned forward. "At least his mama cared enough to be there!"

The horrible accusation seemed to echo forever between them. Meg watched with dread as Jesse laid his fork carefully on the table and stood, his gray eyes dark and stormy.

"I should have followed my first inclination," he hurled at her. "I should have gone to Boston and dragged you home by your hair, if I couldn't make you come any other way."

Meg let out her held breath in a whoosh of surprise. "Then why didn't you?" she whispered.

"Because there didn't seem to be any point," he shot back. "You hadn't learned a damned thing about me or my life or who I am. I don't know who the hell you thought you were marrying—John Wayne, maybe—but it wasn't me." His frustration seemed close to the boiling point.

"Look who's talking!" Her voice trembled. "If you wanted a cowgirl, why were you looking in Aspen, of all places?"

"I *wasn't* looking. You were a complete surprise to me—like a gift from heaven, left under my own personal Christmas tree."

"A gift you unwrapped, used and discarded!"

He flinched. "If that's how you really see it, I was right not to follow you."

He pushed back his chair and stalked out of the room. Shaken, Meg watched him go. Then she buried her face in her hands and tried not to cry.

How would she survive this? He was going to hurt her all over again; she knew it. The attraction he held for her hadn't weakened at all; it had grown stronger and even more dangerous. Maybe she should just offer him a divorce so they could both return to their respective homes and get past all this pain.

No! Clenching her teeth, she dropped her hands to her sides. If he wanted his freedom, let him ask for it. Despite their estrangement, Meg still believed that marriage was forever. There had been no other man for her since Jesse, and there never would be. Even if he should find somebody else—

She swallowed hard and forced herself to face that possibility. *Even if he should find somebody else,* she would never remarry. Therefore, it was pointless to bring up divorce unless…unless he wanted one. Then she'd have no choice but to give it to him. But they would still share a child, and that meant the tie between them could never be truly broken.

Deep in thoughts that depressed her, she cleared the few dishes from the table and straightened the kitchen area. She wouldn't see Jesse again tonight, she was sure of it. He'd stay away until he cooled down, and then he'd refuse to discuss it. The man was stubborn to the bone; how one man could be so unreasonable was beyond her.

This time she wouldn't stand for it. He obviously blamed her for everything and she had a right to know—

The door opened and she jumped a foot. Jesse stood there; he spoke in a low exasperated voice. "If we're going to coexist here for who knows how long, we need to get a few things straight."

Meg spoke around the pulse hammering away in her throat. "I agree." She hesitated, then added suspiciously, "Like what?"

CHAPTER TWO

"WE NEED TO REMEMBER why we're here in the first place." Jesse scowled at Meg. "We'll never get anywhere if we keep sniping at each other. We barely took time to say hello before we started in."

"Why is that, do you suppose?" She meant to say the words sarcastically but they came out with an almost embarrassing bewilderment.

"Who knows?" He shrugged broad shoulders. "We're practically strangers—we haven't met face-to-face in a couple of years."

"Two years, one month and seven days, but who's counting?"

"Thanks for the flash. I needed that kick in the teeth."

"Well, Jesse, what do you expect?" She threw up her hands helplessly. "You've been telling me all along I'm doing a lousy job raising my son—"

"*Our* son! And I said no such—"

"—our son and then expect me to—"

"Meg!"

"—be sweet and reasonable and—"

"Margaret!"

"—and then you get mad and walk out on me and—"

He crossed the room so swiftly that she didn't realize his intent until his hands closed around her upper arms like iron clamps. He lifted her from her chair as if she had no more substance than cotton candy.

Only she did, and her substance was going crazy, choking off her breath and her words and leaving her gasping. He held her still and leaned down to glower into her face. She stared into his long-lashed gray eyes, dizzy with surprise—or something.

"Why are we here?" he demanded, giving her a shake. "Tell me, why are we here?"

"Because we were blackmailed into it! There's absolutely nothing else on earth that could get me here— Let go, Jesse!"

He shook his head and tightened his grip. "That's not the reason. We're here because Randy's in trouble and it's up to us to figure out what to do about it."

"Oh." All the fire went out of her. He was right and the realization humiliated her. She'd gotten so caught up in the past and the present that she'd forgotten about the future. And that was all that counted, really—the future.

He sat her down again and released her. She fell against the backrest of the chair and gazed up at him, wide-eyed, wishing he hadn't touched her. She found herself unconsciously rubbing her arms where his hands had rested, and when she realized what she was doing, yanked her hands away.

He knelt before her, placing his forearms on her knees as if he had every right to do so. She gritted her teeth and tried to think of some suitable comment. Nothing occurred to her.

He let out an explosive breath. "This whole thing has got me locoed," he admitted.

"L-locoed?"

"Crazy. I feel like I've been eatin' loco weed, as Thom T. would say." He shook his head wearily. "Meggie, how the hell did we get into this mess?"

"I...I don't know what you're talking about, Jesse."

"No, I don't suppose you do." His shoulders slumped. "Look, we haven't lived together for five years—yes, I do know how long it's been. Let's give ourselves a few days to get used to each other, okay? Then maybe we can talk about the things we're here to talk about."

She felt the sudden pressure of his arms on her knees as he braced himself to rise, and then he was no longer touching her. She clamped her lower lip between her teeth and sat very still.

"Meggie?"

"Don't call me that!" she burst out.

For a moment she thought he'd retort angrily, but instead he simply shrugged. "Whatever you like, *Meg*. Can we declare a truce for a day or two? We've got a lot of important things to talk about. We can't get hung up on petty bickering."

"Petty bickering," she repeated slowly. "Is that what this is?"

"Looks like it to me, but labels aren't important. What's important is for us to find some common ground. We've got some real major decisions to make, and we'll never be able to make 'em unless we're honest and open with each other."

She didn't like the sound of this at all. *Important things to talk about...major decisions to make... honest and open...*

How could she be honest and open with him? She hadn't even been honest and open with herself, she realized with stunning sadness. If she had, she'd have admitted long ago that he broke her heart when he let her leave without a word. That's what had her so rattled—remembered pain. Thank heaven she'd got over him.

He thrust his hands deep into his pockets. "Don't look at me like I just shot your dog," he complained. "I'm asking for a truce, not a surrender. A temporary ceasefire to see if we can do it—savvy?"

She jerked up straighter in her chair and nodded. "You're right. We need time to get oriented. I don't suppose you're any more prepared for this than I am."

"Less, maybe," he said grimly.

"I doubt that." She arched her brows. "At least we're in your state. Admit it. Texas gives you an edge."

"What difference does it make, whose state we're in?"

"Ask Thom T. and Grandfather—they met halfway, in St. Louis."

"You want to go to St. Louis? Fine! Tomorrow we'll get in my pickup truck and go to St. Louis."

"Why not in my car? Why do we have to go in your pickup?"

"Because your car isn't your car, damn it, it's rented! We'll get in my pickup truck and—"

"Jesse?"

He drew in a quick exasperated breath. "What!"

She smiled. "I think a truce is a wonderful idea."

WHY DO I ALWAYS HAVE to have the last word with him? she wondered as she prepared for bed. *I didn't used to be this way, did I?*

Squeezing toothpaste onto her brush served to remind her that Jesse had always squeezed from the middle of the tube and almost never replaced the cap. Now, she had nice neat tubes of toothpaste, carefully rolled from the bottom and neatly capped.

And she no longer ate beans and wieners or poured sweetened tea down the drain or . . . looked forward to bedtime.

Coming out of the bathroom, she stopped short at the sight of the double bed—not a very big bed, really, not compared to queen-size and king-size. But big enough for two, she knew for a fact.

She sat down disconsolately near the foot of the bed and put an arm around the polished wooden post. She had to sleep here. She had no choice. But seeing the same wedding-ring-patterned quilt, the same crocheted bed skirt, made her want to weep.

It was cruel of their grandfathers to do this, she thought for the dozenth time. Anywhere else—anywhere but here. The path of an erupting volcano would do nicely.

You're being silly, she scolded herself. Jumping to her feet, she threw back the covers, switched off the lamp and bounded into bed. Quivering like a tuning fork, she lay there stiff and unyielding.

I won't sleep a wink tonight, she thought sorrowfully. *I'll be a basket case tomorrow—a basket case on Handbasket Creek.*

And she slept. And she dreamed . . .

Jesse carrying her across the threshold of the family cabin . . . both of them laughing, eager for each other . . . Jesse, sliding her body down his when he stood her on her feet before the fire crackling in the fireplace.

"I love you, Meggie. I never thought I could love anybody the way I love you."

"And I love you, Jesse James Taggart. I'll love you as long as I live."

Exploring, exclaiming over the cabin...drunk with excitement instead of wine...floating from room to room until they reached the final door.

"Oh, Jesse, I've never seen a bed like this."

"It's a marriage bed, Meggie. My great-great-great-grandpa carved the frame himself, and my great-great-great-grandma stitched and stuffed the original feather tick. Thom T. brought my grandma Aggie here on their honeymoon, my father brought my mother and now I've brought you."

Jesse's Stetson, sailing across the room with unerring accuracy to snag on the footpost...Jesse's fingers hot and eager on the buttons of her red traveling suit...Jesse's hands sliding through the waist-length thickness of her hair, spreading it over the down pillow like a veil of silk.

"You have the most beautiful hair in the world, the most beautiful eyes, the most—"

"Wonderful husband. Jesse, promise...we'll always be as happy as we are right...now. Promise me!"

"I promise, love. Anything...anything...oh, yes, anything!"

MEG SAT BOLT UPRIGHT, heart pounding, breathing labored. For a moment she cast about wildly in the darkness for some point of orientation.

And then she realized it was all a dream. No, not a dream, a memory. She slumped back against the pillows and squeezed her eyes closed. The pain he'd brought her later was in direct proportion to the joy he'd brought her first, the old equal-but-opposite re-action.

But he wouldn't get another chance to hurt her, she vowed. Clutching the pillow against her chest, she willed herself to be calm. Maybe she couldn't control her unconscious, but she could control the other aspects of her life. And she would. She would!

She would be pleasant but aloof. She would treat him with distant courtesy. She wouldn't bandy quips with him; she wouldn't argue; she wouldn't pout. She would behave in a polite and civilized manner of which her polite and civilized family would approve.

He would see that here was a woman who would brook no nonsense, she decided, warming to the scenario she was constructing; a woman who had a real handle on life and who was responsible and dedicated and could be trusted to make the right decisions for Randy. Including which school he should attend. Why, this was only the first of many important decisions concerning the boy. If she didn't reach an understanding with Jesse now, they faced *years* of arguments and ugly scenes.

And maybe if they could smooth out their relationship, she would no longer succumb to salacious thoughts about him, even when she was asleep.

Then again, maybe she would.

MEG LOOKED UP from the sausage sizzling in the pan and gave Jesse a reserved smile. "Good morning!" she said with calm authority.

He uttered one word: "Coffee!"

He looked awful. He looked so awful, in fact, that Meg feared her smile might take on a sincerity that would weaken her position of premeditated superiority.

He hadn't shaved and his jaw was stubbly with whiskers. His too-long hair curved around his ears and fell over his forehead, and his eyes were dark with fatigue.

Barefoot, he wore the ubiquitous jeans and a plaid shirt, unbuttoned and hanging open. She watched him pour a cup of coffee and take a big gulp.

And burn his mouth. "Son of a—" he gave her a quick glance and finished "—gun!"

She opened a cabinet and removed a glass. She filled it with water and handed it to him.

"Thanks," he said, and drank.

Now why did I do that? she scolded herself. *He's perfectly capable of taking care of himself. If we start doing favors for each other, it'll be that much harder to keep our distance.*

She realized belatedly that she'd picked up a jar of jam and was struggling to open the lid. When Jesse stepped up close behind her, she felt a physical thrill, although he didn't touch her.

"Let me do that," he said, almost in her ear.

Startled, she let him take the jar from her hands. With a quick flick of his wrist, he opened it, then handed it to her with a somewhat bleak smile.

She took the jar. She could feel herself tensing up because he was standing so close and making her so nervous, and said in a sharp voice, "You look like—" then stopped short.

She wasn't going to do this! She had just promised herself.

"I know," he said glumly. He picked up his mug and carried it to the table. "I look like I've been rode hard and put away wet."

"No, no," she objected hastily, although that certainly was the gist of it. "I was simply going to say, you look... tired."

"I think my mattress is stuffed with rocks." He let his glance run over her, taking his time. "You, on the other hand..."

His leisurely perusal made her wish she hadn't worn such tight jeans, but her jeans choices were limited. Her pale pink T-shirt wasn't tight by any means, but beneath his regard she felt her breasts tighten. To hide her involuntary reaction, she turned away.

He gave an approving grunt. "You, on the other hand, look as if you slept like a baby."

"I did," she lied brightly, grateful for cosmetics, artfully applied. "You know what a comfortable bed that—" Too late she realized her tongue had once again taken a wrong turn. She felt the hot wash of color in her cheeks, and grimaced.

"Yep," he agreed gently. "It's always been a real comfortable bed." His smile looked as if he was finally starting to wake up. "Truce, remember? The last thing I want to do is make you uncomfortable, Meggie—sorry, Meg. So I'll change the subject. What's that great smell in here?"

The spontaneous smile she'd been fighting since he walked into the room finally broke free. "Sausage, gravy and biscuits, with fried eggs on top," she said proudly. "You fixed dinner for me so I'm fixing breakfast for you."

He gave her a startled glance. "But the cook gets to pick the menu."

"That's right." She opened the door of the small oven to check the biscuits browning nicely inside. Using a towel for a pot holder, she extracted the pan.

"But you're cooking my favorite breakfast. If I recall, your favorite is something along the lines of kumquat juice and hummingbird tongues on waffles."

His tone was gently teasing, not goading. Meg wrinkled her nose at him. "Maybe I'm trying to make up for us getting off to such a bad start yesterday. Ever think of that?"

He considered. "Nope," he said finally. "Mainly because you never cooked breakfast for me in your entire life."

"I did so!"

"I said *cooked.* Pouring a bowl of cereal doesn't count. I concede that you did do that once."

"Three times at least." Meg lifted the skillet of gravy off the stove. The truth was, she'd learned to cook only after she left him. It had been something to do while she waited for him to come get her and take her home. She used to fantasize about his surprised delight when he realized how well she'd used their time apart.

You can learn a lot about cooking in five years, she'd discovered.

His voice drifted from behind her as she prepared their plates. "You know, it's a wonder we didn't starve to death. I wouldn't cook and you couldn't cook."

"No, Jesse." She gave him a sweet smile and set his plate in front of him. "I couldn't cook and I knew it. You couldn't cook and didn't know it. It took me a long time to figure that out. Now I *can* cook and you're still deluding yourself. Admit it and I'll give you a biscuit."

SIX BISCUITS LATER, he pushed his plate away with a sigh that could only signify satisfaction. The lavishness of his praise surprised Meg.

"I've never eaten a better biscuit in my life," he concluded, helping her clear the table. "Not even in Texas!"

That made her laugh with both pleasure and surprise. He'd never been generous with his praise. When she did something right—okay, that happened rarely, but it did happen once in a while—he'd shrug it off as if she deserved no particular credit for anything less than a heroic effort.

What he failed to realize, she'd concluded years later, was that all her efforts tended to be heroic. Growing up in a house filled with servants, molded mostly by a grandfather who placed propriety before almost all else, hadn't exactly enhanced her bedmaking, furniture-dusting and carpet-vacuuming skills. She'd been so inept that, after her freshman year at college, she'd moved off campus because she couldn't keep a roommate.

Off campus, she could hire someone to come in regularly to do the hard things—hard things, which included hanging up her clothes and washing dishes.

But she'd learned, proving she could change. Did the fact that he now praised her efforts mean that he, too, had learned while they were apart?

After breakfast and cleanup, Jesse extended a polite invitation to her to go riding with him, and she, just as politely, declined. Things were going very well between them, she thought smugly; better not tempt fate by spending too much time together.

She heard him ride away. When he returned several hours later, she was sitting on the floor before a cold fireplace, a small antique trunk open beside her on the rag rug. An impressive array of old family photographs fanned out around her on the floor.

He walked into the room, and she glanced up with a quick smile. "Look, Jesse," she said softly. "I've found a treasure trove of Taggarts!"

Jesse had never spoken much about his family, but Meg realized now that might have been because she hadn't evinced much interest. The first year of their marriage they'd been totally wrapped up in each other; the second year of their marriage they'd been totally wrapped up in their baby.

The third year of their marriage they'd gotten wrapped up in their differences and never gotten beyond them. The past five years they'd been apart.

She did know the Taggarts were a pioneer Texas family, but little else. Even so, it had never occurred to her that his personal history might be as rich as her own New England heritage—a snobbish attitude that now made her cheeks burn with mortification.

His expression softened as he smiled down at the treasures she'd found. Not all the interesting families came across on the *Mayflower,* Meg thought, whatever Grandfather might believe.

Jesse bent and picked up a picture. "This is Thom T.'s grandmother, Diana," Jesse said, verifying what Meg had concluded from the spidery handwriting on the back of the picture. "She married James Taggart, which explains my middle name. Her people came south after the war."

"The Civil War?"

He grinned. "The War for Southern Rights, or the War between the States or even the War of the Northern Aggression. There was nothing civil about it."

She gave him an impish smile. "Oh, you mean the War of the Southern Rebellion," she suggested brightly.

He raised one skeptical brow, then folded his long legs and sank down beside her. "Where'd you find the trunk?" he asked, patting its peeling leather surface.

"On the floor in the closet. I hope it's okay for me to go through it."

"Sure. We're all Taggarts here."

For the moment, anyway. Meg picked up another photograph and looked into the solemn face of a young woman. She wore a simple dark dress adorned with a magnificent cameo brooch, and even across the decades her eyes sparkled with intelligence.

"That's my great-great-aunt Rose," Jesse said promptly. "She's the one who got tangled up with that famous gunfighter who's buried in the little cemetery in Showdown. The town was plain old Jones, Texas, until my great-great-aunt Rose and her suitors shook things up. There's a whole legend about it."

The woman in the photograph certainly looked as if she could shake up an entire town. There was nothing coy about the way she gazed into the camera lens, an almost smile on her full lips.

"What happened to her?" Meg asked, pleased that the Taggart women could be as rambunctious as the Taggart men.

"Nobody knows for sure," Jesse said solemnly. He seemed to be enjoying her rapt interest. "They say that after the big shoot-'em-up showdown, she ran off with the survivor, who happened to be the sheriff. The good citizens of Jones changed the name of the town to Showdown on the spot to commemorate the most exciting thing that ever happened there.''

Smiling, Meg put the photograph back into the box where she'd found it and began to gather up the others. "How about your great-great-grandmother Diana? What happened to her?"

"She had a happy life," Jesse said. His voice sounded almost mellow, as if talking about his forebears gave him considerable pleasure. "She loved her husband—their marriage lasted something like fifty years. She had three sons, one named Boone who turned out to be Thom T.'s father and my great-grandfather."

Jesse picked up several packets of old letters tied with faded blue ribbons. "I think all the women in my family have been pack rats," he observed. "It's okay to read these if you want to."

"Maybe later." It was hard to force out the words, for Meg was thinking, *fifty years?* Great-great grandpa James must have been a paragon among men, nothing like his independent and hardheaded descendent.

The same descendent who now pulled out a large manila envelope, which she'd hidden at the bottom of a pile of mementos. "What's this?" he asked.

"Nothing," she said hastily, trying to take it from him.

He held it just out of her reach. "If it's nothing, why can't I look?"

"Because—" She bit her lip, watching him open the flap of the envelope and upend the contents onto the floor. "I tried to warn you," she said grimly.

Jesse stared down at the tumble of photos, of himself and Meg and even some of Randy, taken in happier days. Meg, trying to hold Jesse up on the ski slopes...Jesse, trying to teach Meg to saddle a horse...Randy, a wailing smidgin of humanity the day they brought him home from the hospital.

Jesse's glance was sharp. "Did you look at these?"

"No. I mean, I saw what they were and put them aside."

"Why? Are all your memories so bad?"

She started to tell him no, her memories weren't all bad, simply too painful to dredge up. Why be reminded of that time when she'd actually been naive enough to believe he wanted a wife and family? Why be reminded of what she couldn't have?

She might have said those things had she not turned toward him so sharply that they were face-to-face, only inches apart. She looked at him and felt herself sinking into a morass of emotional quicksand.

This was how they'd met, with a shock of recognition and certainty that she'd labeled love at first sight. Jesse's brother, Boone, had been there, too, but she'd hardly even noticed him.

But they'd been young and foolish, and now, she, at least, was neither! She wouldn't fall twice for the smooth brown texture of his skin or the inviting lushness of his dark hair, the subtle curves of his strong mouth, or lashes so long they lay like smudges on his cheeks when he closed his eyes—no!

Jesse's lips flattened into a thin line. "I guess your memories are worse than mine." He swiveled away and shoved the photos back into the envelope. His voice had lost its comfortable edge. "What else did you find?"

"Nothing," she said. "Nothing." She began to thrust things back into the little trunk—pictures, old invitations, recipes, a paper fan embellished with chubby cupids.

He watched without comment. He made no move to stop her when she snatched up the trunk and carried it down the hall.

But when she was out of sight, he slipped the manila envelope from beneath the edge of the rug, where he'd stashed it. Springing to his feet, he carried the envelope into his tiny bedroom and dumped the contents onto the bed.

For a long time he sifted through the photos, occasionally stopping to examine one in detail. Finally all the pictures except one had been returned to the envelope. He picked up the final snapshot and stared at it.

He'd never met a more beautiful girl than Margaret Randall. She'd taken his breath away the first time he'd seen her, with her long mane of honey-gold hair and her brown-velvet eyes. But even so, it wasn't her looks that tripped him up—he'd had his share of beauties but had never even come close to marrying one of them.

No, it was something else—something about her that appealed to him so strongly that all his defenses crumbled. The way she tilted her face to one side when she laughed, the way her eyes widened when she was confused or uncertain, the way she tried to press her soft lips together into a hard line when she was angry.

Everything about her challenged him, drew him in ways he couldn't begin to understand.

Now he found her...the same, only different.

He was getting used to her new short hair, and it seemed to suit her somehow. It brought a softness to her expression—at least, he thought it was the haircut that did that, for she *looked* softer and more feminine than before.

But she wasn't softer. She was harder, and even more stubborn than she'd been when he married her.

What did he expect after five years apart? He tossed the photograph onto the bedside table and lay back on the bed, swinging his booted feet up without regard for the hand-crocheted bedspread. Arms behind his head, he stared bleakly at the ceiling.

This isn't working, he admitted to himself. *I know what those two old fools had in mind, but there's just no chance. They're right about one thing, though—Meg and I can't go on the way we have been.*

It's time to fish or cut bait.

THREE TENSION-PACKED days later, over a dinner of spaghetti with meatballs, he offered her a divorce.

CHAPTER THREE

MEG CHOKED on her red wine and tears sprang to her eyes. When she could breathe again, she clenched her napkin between her hands and glared at Jesse. "*What* did you say?"

"You heard me." He poked at the spaghetti on his plate without enthusiasm. "If you want to file for divorce, I won't fight you."

"How dare you suggest such a thing!" She shoved her plate away and leaned forward, furious with him. "If you want a divorce, get it yourself. And I *won't* cooperate!"

He looked taken aback. "I thought that's what you wanted. Hell, you said yourself you have nothing but bad memories."

"I said no such thing!" She gritted her teeth in frustration. "For your information, I have some very good memories."

"Name a couple."

"Name your own. My good memories are none of your business."

"Why not? I sure as hell get the blame for the bad ones." He sat back in his chair, his face stiff. "I'm trying to be reasonable."

"By saying divorce is the only answer?"

"That's not what I said. It's *one* answer."

"Why are you bringing this up now?" She felt the blood leave her face and a numbing coldness settle in. "Unless..."

"Unless what?"

"There's another woman."

He didn't answer right away, a variety of expressions crossing his face. Was that guilt she saw, or surprise? Shock? Maybe disappointment.

Finally he said in a deadly quiet voice. "I won't dignify that with an answer."

"That's an answer in itself—the same answer I always got from you. Even when I asked how that lipstick got on your collar."

"You didn't ask, you accused. I don't like being crowded."

"And I don't like—" She stopped short. What she didn't like was thinking of him with another woman, but she couldn't very well say that. She finished lamely, "A lot of things."

His expression turned stubborn. "Then you'll file?"

"Absolutely not. That would be like admitting responsibility for the failure of this marriage. I refuse to even consider it. You want a divorce, you file."

"But letting the woman file is the gentlemanly thing to do."

"Well, golly gee, we wouldn't want you to look less than a gentleman." She stood up and snatched her full plate off the table, slopping strands of pasta over the edge. She could barely breathe around the knot in her chest, and her eyes felt hot and dry.

He slumped back in his chair as she began to clean up. With the exception of their first night in the cabin, they'd performed those few chores together. When they'd lived as husband and wife, he'd never helped with the housework, she thought as she banged dishes around. *I hoped we'd both done some growing up while we were apart, but no—he's just the same stubborn, pig-headed, selfish... man he always was.*

He stood up so unexpectedly that Meg dropped a plate. It struck the edge of the counter and fell to the wooden floor, spraying glass shards in all directions.

"The answer," he said, "is no."

She blinked. "The answer to what?"

"To everything." He turned and walked out of the cabin without further explanation.

Her frustration knew no bounds. She wanted to scream, she wanted to cry, she wanted...to know what he meant. No, he wouldn't file for divorce? No, he didn't want a divorce? No, there wasn't another woman?

Or simply no, he wouldn't dignify any of her comments with an answer?

RELATIONS GREW so strained that she was almost glad to see Joe Bob Brooks drive into the clearing a couple of days later. He honked the horn and leaned out the window of his pickup truck.

"Howdy, yawl!" Throwing open the door, he crawled from behind the wheel. Emblazoned on the side of the vehicle was the legend JOE BOB BROOK'S HELL-ON-THE-HANDBASKET GUEST RANCH. Below that, in script, was the slogan Punch a cow with old Joe Bob.

Or punch old Joe Bob himself, Meg thought as she walked down the steps and paused in the shade of a pecan tree, out of the merciless glare of the sun. She didn't miss the flicker of surprise on his face. "Long time, no see," she said cautiously.

"Ain't it the truth!" Joe Bob galloped up to her for all the world like an overgrown puppy dog. He'd gained maybe forty pounds since last she'd seen him, and his belly hung over his fancy belt buckle. He took off his black Stetson and swiped at his face with a forearm, grinning. Dark curly hair tumbled around his chubby face. "J.J. around?"

She gestured vaguely. "Riding."

"Hell of a way to act on a second honeymoon." He gave her a sly wink. "That's what this is, ain't it?"

Meg pasted on a smile. "Gosh, Joe Bob, it sure seems that way, don't it."

"Yeah, well..." He shifted on his booted feet, looking suddenly glum. "Mind if I come in and wait?"

Before she could respond, Meg heard hoofbeats and turned to see Jesse ride into the yard. His buckskin was lathered and skittish, but Jesse sat in the saddle with a negligent grace that was exciting just to watch. His prowess on horseback was legendary, even in a country where children were often set on a horse before they knew how to walk.

A big grin split Jesse's face at the sight of his friend. He waved; the horse shied but his rider went with him, controlling the animal with ease.

"You ol' hoss thief! Why didn't you tell me you was comin' to town?"

"What's the matter, dude-wrangler, your grapevine broken?"

Meg turned away, feeling left out and resentful. Out of the corner of her eye she watched Jesse swing down from the saddle with economical grace, saw the two men shake hands and thump each other happily on the back.

It just wasn't fair for Jesse to have a friend nearby while she had no one. If they were in Massachusetts, it would be the other way around. She wouldn't have cabin fever in her own state.

Was he perhaps breaking the rules? Weren't they supposed to be here together? If he went off with Joe Bob—

Booted feet pounded on the porch, and the two men entered the cabin behind her, Jesse in the lead and Joe Bob at his heels. Their guest did not look happy.

"I don't get it—why won't you come?" Joe Bob demanded.

"I told you," Jesse said reasonably, walking behind the kitchen counter and drawing a glass of water from the tap, "the point of coming here was to spend time with...my wife." He shot her an impassive glance.

"Then why you out ridin' while the little lady waits at the door?" Joe Bob retorted, adding as an aside to Meg, "No offense."

She took none; she was too interested in figuring out what was going on.

Jesse quirked one brow. "You can't think of any possible reason?"

Joe Bob's broad face creased in a frown, then cleared. "You mean you two—" he gestured between them with one finger "—had a little fight, did ya?"

"Jesse and I don't fight," Meg inserted sweetly. "Sometimes we discuss loudly, but we never fight."

A smile tugged at Jesse's mouth and he shrugged.

Joe Bob looked neither convinced nor pleased, but he did look resigned. "Okay, I can take a hint good as the next guy," he grumbled. "You change your mind, you know where to find me." He turned toward the door. "Guess I might's well leave you two *lovebirds* alone."

"Sorry, buddy."

"How about the Fourth of July shindig? You're comin' to that, ain't you? We don't put on the dog like they do in Showdown, but everybody in Hell's Bells is a-fixin' to celebrate. Fireworks, games, the whole enchilada—bring Maggie, why don'cha?"

"Meg. Her name's Meg."

"Whatever," Joe Bob said carelessly as the two men moved through the doorway. "Gonna have chili and barbecue and ice cream—"

"You bringin' your dudes in to partake of a real Texas Fourth of July?"

"Guests, J.J. Guests. They don't like bein' called dudes anymore."

The two men passed out of earshot and Meg sat down glumly at the table and picked up her paperback book. She'd read page twenty-three at least five times and still didn't know what the story was about. She was bored; she was sick of her own company; she was going stir-crazy! If Joe Bob had invited her to a pig-sticking—whatever that might be—she'd have jumped at the chance to get away from here for a while.

Jesse stuck his head through the doorway. "You got fifteen minutes," he announced.

"For what?"

"To get ready to go into town with me."

"To do what?"

He grinned, the grin that always did such nice things to an already nice face. "Does it matter?"

"I guess not," she admitted breathlessly.

"Yep, that's how I feel, too. I've got to cool down the buckskin and then we can go. Meet me out front?"

Yes, yes, yes, yes, yes!

THEY LEFT THE CABIN shortly before noon, driving away with all the windows rolled down in the pickup and the radio blaring a country-and-western lament.

"We could use a few things from the grocery store," Meg observed after a while, above the music and the roar of the engine.

Jesse downshifted over a particularly deep rut in the dirt road. "Figured that'd be our last stop." He steered onto the paved two-lane road and the noise level subsided considerably.

Meg leaned back against the bench seat. "This is a good idea."

"Yep. I'd think we were suffering from too much togetherness except we've hardly been together at all the last couple of days."

"Meals—if you can count sitting at the same table and ignoring each other being together."

He gave her a quick glance. "If we ever expect to get our sentence commuted, we've got to start talking. You know that, don't you?"

"Yes." She tightened her lips, looking down at her hands clutched in her lap. "But it's hard!" she burst out. "That cabin has so many memories—most of them good, I hasten to add. But I'm finding it hard to get past...everything."

"Me, too." He kept his attention straight ahead on the road. His face in profile looked tense but determined. "That's water under the bridge," he said finally. "We've got to concentrate on what happens next."

"I know you're right. For Randy's sake..."

"Yes. For Randy's sake." After a moment, he added, "You know what they're hoping for, of course."

She'd been staring at him, and when he turned his head he caught her at it. She looked away guiltily. "Who?"

"The grandpas."

"Oh. Well, it's obvious. They're...they're hoping we'll quit fighting over our son."

He slowed for a right-hand turn. The town of Hell's Bells lay ahead down the tree-lined road. "Yep. And they figure the best way to get us to do that is to put this marriage back together again. Reconciliation, Meg."

The shock of hearing that word said aloud left her flabbergasted. "They're crazy!"

"Like a couple of foxes. Why else would they force us to hole up in the cabin where we spent our honeymoon? Why else would they sprinkle pictures of happy times around—and they did. You find one of our wedding pictures in the big bedroom?"

Meg swallowed hard. "Yes. You too?"

"Yep." He gave a disgusted shake of his shaggy head. "Thom T. told me it was time to stand up and be counted. Either the marriage is on or it's off. If it's off..."

She knew the word he didn't say this time: divorce. "What did you tell him?" she demanded, feeling her temper rise.

"That it's none of his damned business and we'll do what we please."

"Good for you!"

They glared at each other, because the two old men weren't handy to take the heat they'd generated.

Jesse steered the truck into the parking lot of the Lone Star Texasburger Drive Inn, maneuvered into a parking space next to a speaker for placing orders and killed the engine. "'Course for all I knew, you wanted a divorce. That's why I brought it up before, in case you were too...shy...embarrassed...whatever, to mention it."

She didn't know whether to thank him for his thoughtfulness or blast him for his presumption. She decided on a middle course. "If I wanted a divorce I certainly would have—"

"Howdy, yawl!" The speaker on a pole next to the open window squawked. "That you in that pickup, J.J. Taggart? Welcome home, honey!"

Jesse turned toward the speaker box. "Ida Mae Tuttle, you still fryin' hamburgers after all these years?"

Static distorted the woman's chortle. "Them's *Texasburgers,* honey, not them puny little ol' thangs other folks sell. Say, who you got out there with you in that pickup truck? Is that Carter Dobbins's oldest gal?"

Meg, who'd been listening to the exchange with a smile on her face, felt her good humor evaporate. She didn't know who Carter Dobbins's "oldest gal" was, but apparently she was no stranger to Jesse.

He gave Meg a self-conscious glance before returning to his conversation with the disembodied voice of Ida Mae Tuttle. "Get your foot out of your mouth, Ida—I got my wife with me."

"Oops! Sorry 'bout that. I'll bring your usual for two—Texasburgers 'n' fries, comin' right up."

The speaker went dead. "I'm sorry," Jesse said, looking as if he meant it. "You do sorta look like Carter's oldest girl, at least from a distance."

"How flattering," she said coolly.

"Should be. Donna Dobbins always was the prettiest girl in town, at least until you—" He stopped short and drew a quick breath. "Forget Donna Dobbins. Meg, I never wanted to hurt you."

"Being mistaken for Donna Dobbins can hardly be painful to me," she said stiffly.

"That's not what I mean and you know it." He took off his hat and tossed it onto the seat between them, where it lay like a fence. "I mean ever. Any hurt I caused you wasn't done out of malice. Ignorance, maybe, stupidity... not malice."

Meg brushed the hat brim with tentative fingers. Touching his hat was almost like touching the man, it was so much a part of him. She pulled her hand away. "I never meant to hurt you, either," she murmured. "I mean, I *did,* after you hurt me first, but it wasn't really personal. It was more like...self-defense. Does that make sense?"

"No," he said gravely, "but I catch your drift."

"Do you?" She couldn't believe it when she heard herself challenge him. Why couldn't she learn to leave well enough alone? "You didn't catch my drift the other day when I was looking at the things in the trunk." He hadn't caught her drift when she'd packed up their child and walked out on him, but she wasn't emotionally prepared to go into that now.

Maybe not ever.

"Didn't it occur to you—"

"Hey, roll up your window a smidge so's I can put on the tray!"

They both jumped and shifted toward the driver's window, where a middle-aged matronly face beamed at them. Jesse adjusted his window and Ida Mae slipped the tray onto the side of the vehicle as if she'd done it a thousand times, which very likely she had.

She looked past Jesse to Meg. "Howdy," she said politely. "I'm Ida Mae Tuttle and I've known this boy since he was a pup."

Meg smiled back, enjoying the woman's open friendliness. "I'm pleased to meet you. I'm—"

"Ever'body in town knows about J.J.'s pretty little wife. I was only jokin' before," Ida Mae interrupted. "You kids stayin' at the cabin, right?"

"That's right." Jesse took a cardboard basket of French fries from the tray and would have placed it on top of his hat had Meg not snatched it aside. He seemed somehow distracted.

"Real nice spot for a second honeymoon." Ida Mae winked. "Maybe I'll see you at the big Fourth of July shindig." She bounced away.

Meg reached for a French fry, burned her fingers and let it drop back into the basket. "What's all this about a second honeymoon everybody seems to be talking about?" she asked crossly.

Jesse picked up both enormous hamburgers and handed one to her. "Apparently that's the story Thom T. put out. I suppose he thought he was doing us a favor."

"Oh, really?"

"Hey, lighten up. What was he supposed to say? That we needed a place to go a few rounds to decide whether or not to kill each other? At least the word 'honeymoon' tends to keep people away."

"All except Joe Bob." Somewhat mollified, Meg took a tentative bite of her Texasburger. It had mayonnaise, lettuce and tomato on it, and several whole gherkin pickles about the size of her little finger. Strange, she thought, very strange. But not bad.

He lifted the plastic catsup dispenser off the tray. "Joe Bob knew us as a couple a lot better than anybody else around here did." He aimed a squirt of soupy red catsup at the basket of fries. "I don't think he bought the second-honeymoon story."

"Or if he did, ignored it."

"Hey, cut the guy some slack, why don't you? His marriage just fell apart and he's working thirty-six hours a day to make the dude ranch pay. He's got troubles of his own."

"I stand corrected," she said meekly but didn't mean it. She was sorry the guy'd lost his wife, but she couldn't imagine any woman willing to put up with his incessant practical jokes and his male chauvinist tendencies.

They finished their lunch companionably enough, talking about the weather and the town and the people but not about themselves. After Jesse carried the tray in to Ida Mae, they drove to the Yellow Rose Grocery Store, a mom 'n' pop operation, and went inside. The cabin had been well stocked, but they chose a few fresh items—milk, fruit.

"Hear yawl on your second honeymoon," the grocery checker remarked as she punched prices into the cash register. "Lawdy, how time flies!"

"You got that right," Jesse agreed, and Meg could see a smile twitch the corners of his mouth.

"That was fun," Meg told him later as they carried the three bags of groceries into the cabin. "I feel a lot more relaxed. I think I was getting tired of my own company."

"Me, too." He stood at the end of the kitchen counter and watched her put away their supplies. "I'm sorry about that."

She picked up a plastic bag of bananas. "About what?"

"Leaving you to your own devices for the past few days. I...had to get a few things straight in my mind."

"And you were able to do that?" Her voice sounded too wistful for comfort.

"I think so. It seems to me we've got to forget about the hurt feelings and the accusations we're trying not to make and the slights we've been nursing. Clear the slate, start fresh."

Meg considered. In a way, he could be right. It might be possible, on a superficial level, to simply ignore the deeper differences between them. If they were trying to put something together again, something lasting, it wouldn't work. But he wasn't asking for that, he obviously didn't want that, any more than she did.

So why not make it as easy on herself as she could? If she tucked away her real feelings somewhere deep inside, she could enjoy—no, tolerate!—his companionship on an impersonal level. She could let herself become acclimatized to him again just to the point where they could talk reasonably about their son's future.

They'd gotten off to a rocky start but survived it. Neither one of them had walked out because the stakes were too high. What would it do to their son's life if his parents couldn't find some way to accommodate each other?

"Okay," she said. "Clear the slate. Try again." She gave a nervous little laugh. "All this 'try, try again' stuff goes against my natural inclinations, but I suppose...for Randy..."

"Aw, Meggie."

The new sad note in his voice brought her head swinging up. He stepped forward and put his hands on her shoulders, lightly, yet with dramatic repercussions. Time seemed to stand still. All she could do was stare at him, her heart in her throat, intensely aware of a throbbing warmth where he touched her.

The corners of his wide sensuous mouth curved up in a smile. "We'll both do it for Randy. We'll force ourselves to come back and keep coming back until we finally figure out what's best for him. We may bleed before this is over. We may wish we'd never laid eyes on each other. But we'll do what we must—for Randy."

He pulled her into his arms and she allowed it, too shocked to protest. It had been so long, so very long. She stood there rigidly, feeling the beat of his heart, smelling the clean outdoors scent of him. Dizzy with a heady mixture of fear and anticipation, she fought to keep her arms stiff at her sides.

He pressed her head into the curve beneath his chin, and she felt more than heard his sigh, so bittersweet that she began to tremble.

His whisper stirred the hair at her temple. "We're in this together, you know. We made a baby together and we'll never be able to break that connection."

"Jesse..." Her voice betrayed her.

"I know, I know."

He tightened his arms around her so unexpectedly that she gasped. She felt his lips brush the top of her head—and then he set her aside, his arms falling away. On her own again, she swayed.

His crooked smile cut through subterfuge like a laser. "I presume too much," he said. "I always have. But I thought if I touched you, you would feel my sincerity. Trust me, Meg. Trust me. I won't hurt you again."

Dared she believe? He stood before her, solid and real and oh, so appealing. She searched his face for any indication of deceit and found none. Remembering what it had felt like to be in his arms again, she shivered.

"I guess I have to trust you," she said slowly. "There doesn't seem to be any other way if we're going to work this out."

But I'm only doing it for Randy.

MEG SAT ON THE SOUTH BANK of Handbasket Creek, leaning dreamily against the gnarled roots of an old tree and listening to the chink of bridles and the creak of saddle leather. She probably shouldn't have given in to temptation and agreed to come riding with Jesse. She probably should have turned him down firmly but courteously when he suggested it.

But she hadn't. Heaven help her, she hadn't.

"Easy, boy."

Behind her, Jesse's voice gentled the horses as easily as it gentled her nerves. She curved her arms behind her head and closed her eyes. Listening to the hum of insects and the songs of birds, she savored the sultry heat.

Suspended somewhere between fantasy and reality, she sighed. The days had gotten better but the nights were worse. She'd thought she'd get used to sleeping in *that* bed in *that* room once the unhappy tension eased.

She'd been wrong.

Another kind of tension was building, a kind even harder to handle. Everything seemed to conspire to remind her of past happiness.

The operative word was "past"—memories, nothing more, she assured herself again and again. Granted, Jesse was the only man she'd ever loved, but that had ended a long time ago. She *couldn't* have feelings for him now; they'd been apart too long, and the things that had driven them apart still stood between them.

She recited the litany of his sins in her mind: he had unrealistic expectations of marriage and of her; he never explained anything; he never took her feelings into consideration; he...

She caught and held a deep breath. *Cut to the chase,* she ordered herself. *Jesse never really needed me then, and he sure doesn't need me now.* That's what it all came down to in the end. That's what all the rest of it added up to.

She needed to be needed. That's why she taunted and tormented him. If ever once he told her he couldn't live without her—

"Shh!"

There was a stir of movement and a hand covered her mouth. She opened her eyes wide, heart leaping with alarm. Jesse crouched beside her, his face only inches from hers. She could see the smile in his gray eyes and the arch of his dark brows. A strange sweet lassitude flowed through her. Beneath his gentle fingers, her lips parted in a smile of surprised delight.

"Don't make a sound. Just turn your head slowly toward the creek."

With his hand, he gently guided her. She offered no resistance, incapable at that moment of independent thought or action.

His breath in her ear sent a shudder rippling through her. She eased to her knees, trying to concentrate, but he was too close and she was too aware of him. He leaned forward, his chest pressing against her back while his arm slid around her middle with a thrilling intimacy.

"Do you see it?" He raised his other arm slowly to point.

She didn't at first. All she could see was the creek flowing lazily past, the low bank on the opposite side, trees crowding almost to the water's edge . . .

And the deer, muzzle thrust into the creek as it drank. Meg stiffened and caught her breath, leaning forward slightly. She risked a quick glance over her shoulder. "Bambi!" She mouthed the word, and he nodded.

As she watched, her enchantment grew. There seemed something magical about the combination: sylvan setting, delicate wild creature and the elemental force of the man surrounding her physically and emotionally.

The deer flung up its head as if aware of the strange electric charge in the air. It was so near Meg could see the spray of water from its muzzle, the flare of its nostrils. The great dark eyes met hers in an instant of understanding quickly replaced by alarm. Whirling, the deer bounded gracefully away between the trees.

Meg let out her breath in a soft sigh and slumped back against Jesse's chest. Her arms covered his, still about her waist.

"That was a white-tailed deer," Jesse whispered, his lips brushing her earlobe. "We've got a lot of 'em here in the Hill Country. Farther west they have mule deer, also called—" he slid one hand up her midriff, fingers splayed "—black-tailed deer."

She let her head fall onto his shoulder, because she lacked the strength not to. He held her there for a moment before lowering her back against the tree trunk. Eyes wide, she waited for whatever was to come. Nothing seemed real, which made it possible for her to float on a cloud of make-believe.

"Just once," he said in a rough-edged voice. "Just once," he repeated more strongly. "I've got to know if I'm crazy or if your lips really are as sweet as I remember."

"Jesse, you mustn't!" As he leaned toward her she lifted her hands to brace against his chest, meaning to hold him away. But the magic of the moment proved too strong; she curled her fingers into his shirt and drew him down.

Their lips met in an incredible burst of excitement. The feelings rushing over her were too strong—she gave herself up to the intoxicating power of his kiss. A melting languor flowed through her, into every extremity, leaving her weak and trembling.

He drew back and they stared into each other's eyes. He looked as astonished as she felt.

He shoved a hand through his hair, the movement uncharacteristically jerky. "Look," he said in an unsteady voice, "we're about to dive into some deep waters here. We need a time-out, some kind of distraction while we get our bearings. Want to go into Hell's Bells for the big Fourth of July celebration?''

Today is the Fourth of July? Terrific, she thought. *I almost gave in on Independence Day!*

CHAPTER FOUR

EVERY SINGLE RESIDENT of Hell's Bells seemed to be streaming into town by the time Jesse found a parking place. "It'll be a bit of a walk to the rodeo grounds," he told Meg. "I don't think we can get much closer."

Those were the first words to pass between them since they'd climbed into the pickup truck to head for town. Her response was stiff. "That's all right. I don't mind walking."

He opened his door and jumped out, hurrying around to give her a hand. Knowing he would, she climbed down from the cab on her own before he could reach her. "Now what?" she asked cautiously.

He shrugged. "Follow the crowd."

That wasn't difficult to do. Everyone in town and for miles around must have been there, Meg decided as she and Jesse crossed the unpaved parking area, really just an empty lot. Kids and dogs ran around and between adults, people waved and called out to their friends and chased their children, riders on horseback threaded their way cautiously through the mass of humanity. Nobody seemed to mind the bedlam. In fact, everyone seemed to be enjoying themselves enormously.

There must be a million dollars' worth of boots and denim in town today, Meg decided as they fell in with the crowd flowing toward the small rodeo arena southeast of the town proper. A few of the women wore sundresses and sandals, as did she, while some of the younger girls and children wore shorts. But the uniform of choice was jeans, boots, fancy western shirts and Stetson hats.

Nobody wore that outfit better than Jesse. She stole a glance at him, just as he looked down at her.

"Friends?" he asked in a cautious voice.

"I wish!" She spoke ruefully. If he were her friend, she surely wouldn't feel this incredible physical attraction. Yes, she could admit it here in the safety of an impersonal crowd: physical attraction. After sharing that kiss on the creek bank, how could she deny it? Friendship would be a glorious relief. You could even love a friend without putting your very existence in danger, right?

"Pretend, then." He took her elbow and guided her across a broken patch of sidewalk. "Hey, loosen up." He gave her stiff arm a gentle shake. "We're here to get away from our troubles and have a little fun."

"Heaven knows we both need to do that."

"You got that right."

She stopped walking and faced him, planting her hands on her hips. The crowd obligingly flowed around them. "So this is your turf. What do we do first?"

"This." He led her to a booth where the Hell's Bells volunteer fire department offered helium-filled balloons.

"Howdy, J.J.," the rotund gentleman behind the counter greeted, smiling at Meg. "How's yore granddaddy?"

Jesse, allowing that his granddaddy was mighty fine, bought Meg three balloons: one red, one white and one blue. They hadn't proceeded a block before she spotted a boy of perhaps four, clinging to his mother's skirt and wistfully eyeing the colorful balloons. He was an adorable child in miniature jeans and boots, inexplicably reminding her of Randy.

She smiled and he smiled back shyly. She caught Jesse's elbow to get his attention. "Do you mind?" she asked, indicating the balloons and nodding toward the boy.

His glance followed hers and he smiled at the child, then at the mother. "Howdy, Donna," he greeted. "Okay if we give ol' Hopalong here some balloons?"

The child's mother looked around and saw Jesse. "Jesse James Taggart!" she exclaimed, opening her arms flirtatiously. "I heard you's back in town! Give me a hug, stranger!"

Jesse darted Meg a what-can-I-do? glance and stepped forward to meet the enthusiastic advances of the woman who could only be Carter Dobbins's oldest girl, Donna. *We don't look a thing alike,* Meg assured herself as she watched Donna's flirtatious manner. *She's much... flashier.*

"I don't believe you've met my friend, Billy Ray Risley." Donna indicated the lanky cowboy standing beside her. He stepped forward, expression testy but hand extended. "Billy Ray's from Waco."

Jesse shook the proffered hand. "Jesse Taggart. This is my wife, Meg." He drew her to his side.

Billy Ray's frown disappeared. "Proud to know you," he said to Jesse, his nod including Meg. "Seen you ride in Houston a while back. Don't know how you ol' boys keep takin' that kind of punishment." He shook his head in admiration.

"Smart ones don't," Jesse said. "Don't mean to hold you folks up..." The crowd had become thicker and someone bumped into Meg, throwing her momentarily off balance. Jesse slipped an arm around her waist protectively. "We're gonna get run over if we don't get out of the way, here. Meggie just wanted to give the boy her balloons, if that's all right."

Donna smiled at Meg. "That's real nice." She put her hand on the child's shoulder. "Shane, you want the lady's balloons? Say 'please' to Miz Taggart."

"Please," Shane said, then hid his face against his mother's leg.

Meg knelt before him, aware when Jesse positioned himself to shield her from the crowd. She held out her offering. "I have a little boy of my own who likes balloons," she said gently.

"Where is your little boy?" the child asked, reaching for the prize.

"Visiting his grandfather." She swallowed back the lump in her throat, carefully transferring the strings confining the helium-filled balloons from her hand to his small grubby one. "Hang on tight so they won't get away from you." She pressed a kiss on his chubby cheek and stood up quickly.

With waves and smiles, she and Jesse moved back into the mainstream. She heard the boy call, "Hey, thanks, lady," and his mother's admonishment, "That's *Miz* Taggart, Shane."

Somehow, the brief encounter buoyed her spirits, and for the first time Meg found herself actually anticipating the day ahead. She hugged tight against Jesse's arm for protection from the crowd, and her step grew lighter. He gave her a puzzled glance but said nothing.

As they entered the picnic grove next to the rodeo grounds, a voice called Meg's name. Surprised, she looked around to see Laurel Anderson, the clerk from the convenience store, hurrying up.

Laurel dismissed Jesse with a friendly "Howdy, J.J.," and smiled at Meg. "How's it goin'?" she asked.

Meg smiled back; it would have been impossible not to. "Very well, thank you. Obviously, Hell's Bells is the place to be on Independence Day." She indicated the crowd milling about and the abundant red-white-and-blue bunting adorning every structure, post and tree.

"It ain't up to what they do in Showdown but it ain't bad. So where yawl sittin'? If you don't have plans, join me and my brood—kids and grandkids both. Our blanket's over there close to the bandstand. Speeches'll be startin' in a while—don't want to miss that." She winked and laughed.

Meg looked inquiringly at Jesse.

"She's pullin' your leg," he said with a smile. "The local politicians practically have to pay people to listen to them." He dropped an arm easily around Meg's shoulders. "We'll look you up later," he told Laurel, "if you promise to save me a piece of that pecan pie of yours."

"I do that every year, but you hardly ever come around to collect it. I got three, four pieces of that stuff petrifyin' in my kitchen!" Laughing, she waved them on their way.

"I like her," Meg said as Jesse guided her through the crowd. "She's nice."

"Most Texans are, if you give 'em half a chance."

She darted him a quick glance. His expression remained innocent—too innocent. "True. So are most Bostonians," she said lightly, realizing they'd both spoken the truth.

The sound of music caught their attention and they paused to listen. A lot of power could be generated by two middle-aged men with guitars and a boy with a banjo, Meg discovered. Most of the tunes she'd never heard before, although a couple of folk songs stirred faint memories.

For some reason, though, their music went straight to her heart. Soon she, who considered the Boston Pops just about as folksy as she cared to get, was tapping her toe and clapping along with everybody else. The enthusiasm of the crowd in turn spurred the entertainers to ever greater efforts. They finished with a dazzling burst of dexterity that left the audience cheering and the performers red-faced and grinning.

"That was wonderful!" Meg exclaimed. She leaned against Jesse's arm and looked up at him with amazement. It seemed somehow important to share the moment.

"It can be," he agreed.

"Are they professionals?" It never occurred to her to release her hold on him as they walked toward the food booths ahead.

"Nope. They play for the love of it. One sells insurance, one's the local pharmacist and the boy's going to college."

"Majoring in music, I hope."

Jesse shook his head. "Majoring in engineering. His girlfriend doesn't want him to be a musician, I hear.

Afraid he'll have to fight the girls off with a stick—and what if he broke his stick?''

"Waste all that talent because— Why, that's the silliest—!'' She saw the laughter in his eyes and broke off, suddenly embarrassed.

Girls liked cowboys, too.

"Over here, yawl!''

It was Joe Bob, standing beside a booth that proclaimed, The World's GREATEST Chili!!! His once-white apron looked as if it had survived an explosion in a lunchroom, but his tall chef's hat, unsullied, bent at a jaunty angle.

Joe Bob leaned over an enormous iron pot suspended above a wood fire, waving a long-handled spoon enthusiastically to get their attention. Close to a dozen men and women clustered around him, watching the proceedings with interest and much friendly camaraderie.

I'm not going to let Joe Bob ruin my day, Meg vowed, following Jesse toward the booth. Not this time!

"Take a whiff,'' Joe Bob invited, stirring the contents of the pot with great sweeping strokes. "This has gotta be the best chili ever made.''

Obediently Meg and Jesse sniffed the heady aroma—sniffed and, in Meg's case, recoiled. If the very air was spicy enough to bring tears to her eyes, what would a bite of that stuff do to her? She was afraid to find out!

Jesse was made of sterner stuff. "I don't know,'' he said, shaking his head as if weighing pros and cons. "I'd have to taste it to be certain.''

"Sure thing.'' Joe Bob turned his head toward the booth and called, "Suzi? We got a volunteer taster over here. Bring me one a'them cups, will you, honey?"

"Suzi's my assistant," Joe Bob explained with a wink for Jesse. "She's one'a the 'guests' at the ranch and she likes hangin' out with cowboys."

Meg could see why he didn't mind obliging the lovely Suzi, who sashayed through the ranks with a stack of paper cups in one porcelain-nailed hand and several plastic spoons in the other. Like most everyone else in sight, she wore cowboy clothes. Unlike most everyone else in sight, hers were tight to the point of strangulation. Her shiny stretch pants fit like a tourniquet, and the pearl snaps on her semi-sheer shirt were unfastened several notches south of all reason.

Suzi tossed her blond Hollywood-starlet mane and gave Jesse a simmering look. "How-dee, shu-gah," she drawled. "Ah'm up fer a part in a biiiig Hollywood movie and ah'm a-practicin' mah Tax-us accent. How'm I doin', you-all?"

Joe Bob snatched the cups from her. "Not too damned good, *shu-gah.*" He ladled out a lethal-looking portion of chili and handed it to Jesse, pointedly ignoring Meg.

Suzi pouted and stamped one foot, calling attention to long thin legs and boots with three-inch heels. "Nuts," she said. "I've been practicing. I thought this time I had it cold."

"The accent's harder than most people think," Jesse offered politely, looking from the cup in his hand to the spoons still clutched in Suzi's.

"Fer sure!" Suzi sounded relieved to find someone who understood her problems. "I mean, you guys are like, *hard.*" She giggled, her blue eyes opening wide.

"I mean, your *accent* is hard, and I'm a *professional*."

"Right on all counts, honey." Joe Bob smirked and took the spoons from her. "Trot your buns back behind that counter and finish up that sign you been workin' on all day. This stuff is ready for my adorin' public! Am I right, J.J.?"

Jesse gave Joe Bob a hard look, then flashed an apologetic glance at the two women. Maneuvering a big glob of steaming chili onto his spoon, he offered it to Meg. "Honey?"

Meg, who'd been watching Joe Bob and Suzi with a kind of morbid fascination, smiled at her husband. "Thanks but no thanks—I'll pass. I'm a coward. I admit it." She thought she heard a murmur of approval from the crowd.

"Okay, then, here goes."

Jesse lifted the spoon, looked at the contents carefully, then inserted it into his mouth. He tasted, making a great show of it, cocking his head from one side to the other, nodding, frowning, narrowing his eyes. Meg almost laughed aloud, watching Joe Bob shift anxiously from one foot to the other.

"Well?" the big man burst out as if overcome by the suspense. "What's the verdict?"

Jesse took his time. "Joe Bob...I can say...without fear of contradiction, I can say...this chili is...the best you ever made."

Joe Bob let out his breath in a gusty sigh of triumph. "Hear that?" he exclaimed to no one in particular. "Hot damn!"

"Except..."

The single word was a bucket of cold water on Joe Bob's elation. "Except! What's that supposed to mean—except?"

"Joe Bob, you're hollerin' like a stuck pig," Jesse said calmly, taking another bite of chili. He swallowed before going on. "Best you ever made, except maaaaybe it's just a tad too tomato-ey."

"What? What!" Joe Bob's face turned bright red and he took a swing at Jesse with the wooden spoon.

Laughing, Jesse easily avoided his friend's ire. Grabbing Meg's hand, he pulled her through the crowd—through the crowd and straight to a stand that sold beer. He chugalugged half a paper cupful of the brew before pausing to draw a deep breath.

"That stuff's hot enough to scorch your tonsils," he gasped. "Joe Bob may really have gone too far this time. Some dude tries to eat it and he'll need a mouth transplant."

He offered Meg a drink from his cup, and after a brief hesitation, she accepted. Never a big fan of beer, she took a single swallow, more as a friendly gesture than for any other reason.

"Why didn't you tell him the chili was too hot instead of talking about tomatoes?" she asked.

Jesse shoved his hat onto the back of his head. Picking up a paper napkin from the beer counter, he swiped at his damp forehead. "Couple of reasons. Number one, he *wanted* me to say it was too hot so he could lord it over me."

Meg shook her head in mock disapproval. "Men!"

"What can I say?" He finished his beer and tossed the cup into a trash receptacle.

"What's the other reason?" She let him take her arm and guide her toward the rodeo arena.

"Joe Bob's told everybody for years that he uses special imported tomatoes to make his chili so good— goes on and on about it to anybody who'll listen. Truth is, he doesn't use any tomatoes at all. Or any of the other off-the-wall stuff he claims he puts in, like rattlesnake meat and possum gizzards and—"

"*Possum* gizzards?"

"A figure of speech." He hauled her snugly against his side to let a knot of giggling teenaged girls pass. "A genuine dude will believe anything—hell, a *Texan* will believe anything when it comes to chili or barbecue. Some kind of mystique, I reckon."

They reached the tall wire fence around the rodeo arena and stopped. Far to the right were the chutes from which cowboys and animals emerged; closer to the left were the holding pens where the animals exited. People wandered in and out of the small bleacher section to watch the men and boys fooling around in the arena.

"Will there be a rodeo later?" Meg asked, wondering why he hadn't come prepared for that eventuality.

He shook his head, his attention centered on activity near the chutes. "Haven't had any real rodeos in Hell's Bells in years. The guys just like to come down here and fool around. Kind of like sandlot ball."

A sorrel horse broke from the roping chute. Even to Meg's untutored eye, it looked like trouble on the hoof. The rider, a kid of perhaps fifteen or sixteen, sawed on the reins, elbows and heels flapping as he tried to regain the upper hand. The horse headed straight for the closed gate at the end of the arena, gaining speed with every moment.

"Son of a…!" Jesse jumped and caught the top of the fence with his hands, thrusting the sharp toes of his

boots into the mesh. "That damned mule-headed..."
He cast a tense glance at Meg. "He's got the bit in his
teeth. Damn!"

A collective gasp arose from the audience as the
horse careered forward. At the last possible instant,
the animal veered left, scraping his rider's leg against
the fence but sparing him the head-on crash that had
seemed inevitable.

Tossing his head, the horse came on around the
curve and raced back in the opposite direction, refus-
ing to be controlled. Meg had just a glimpse of the
boy's white face; he was scared and who could blame
him? But he was also embarrassed and humiliated,
and he sawed viciously at the reins and jammed the
blunt rowels of his spurs into the horse's flanks. Flecks
of foam flew from the sorrel's muzzle, and Meg could
see the whites of his eyes as he raced past.

Jesse released his hold on the fence and dropped
lightly onto the ground beside Meg. "Billy Vaughn's
a damned fool to let Little Billy ride that half-broke
bronc," he blazed. "That horse is crazy to start with,
but he's still got more sense than Little Billy." He
grabbed her hand. "Come on."

He started off toward the chutes at a fast walk, but
after only a few steps he broke into a trot. Grateful for
flat-heeled sandals, Meg kept pace—but just barely.
Past the grandstands they hurried, and around back,
where Jesse stopped so abruptly that Meg plowed into
him.

People milled about mostly on foot but a few on
horseback. For a moment Meg couldn't see what had
arrested Jesse's attention. Then she heard the sharp
crack of a blow and saw Little Billy still astride the red

horse. The boy raised his arm high, a quirt with a braided leather lash in his hand.

The sorrel trumpeted his rage and reared. People scattered like leaves in a windstorm, trying to escape the flashing hooves. Taken by surprise, the boy toppled backward. The riderless horse came down running—just as a group of children swarmed around a corner, herded by their mothers.

Meg screamed and threw herself toward the children. She recognized Donna Dobbins's little boy, Shane, in the lead, his chubby face frozen in fear and confusion. She whirled around with arms spread wide, as if she could shield him and the other children from harm.

The sudden realization that Jesse was not beside her sent a shaft of pure terror knifing through her. Then she saw he'd launched himself to meet the charge of the wild-eyed horse.

For one heart-stopping instant she thought the crazed red animal would grind the man beneath its pounding hooves. At the last possible moment, Jesse hurled his lithe body at the horse's head. One arm swept over the animal's eyes and yanked the big head down. With his other hand, Jesse grabbed the bridle and hung on, digging his boot heels into the soft earth as if bulldogging a steer.

The horse's own momentum swung it around in a circle. Blinded by Jesse's arm, confused and terrified, the animal stumbled and went to one knee. At that moment, Jesse grabbed a handful of mane and vaulted into the saddle.

A ragged cheer startled Meg from her trance. A quick glance told her the children had retreated around the corner of the fence, out of harm's way. Now only

Jesse mattered—Jesse, the first man she'd ever loved, the man she still loved. She pressed her knuckles against her mouth to keep from crying out in fear for him.

Fear for Jesse, who didn't need it. Jesse, the ultimate cowboy, as at home in the saddle as if he'd invented it. The horse began to buck and Jesse flowed with him, taking everything the long-legged sorrel could throw. The horse didn't stand a chance. Jesse seemed to anticipate every trick, moving with easy grace to counter it.

Someone with presence of mind opened the big gate to the arena and Jesse yanked the head of the bucking horse around. A few more stiff-legged crow-hops and horse and rider were safely inside.

So the emergency was over. But when the mounted pickup man rode near to take Jesse off, the crowd let out a collective wail, "Ride 'em, cowboy!" a youthful voice sang out, and others picked up the chant.

Meg scrambled up to perch on top of the rail fence near the chutes. She saw Jesse's head go back and his teeth flash in a white smile. With a quick twist of his wrist, he wrapped both reins in one hand. Yanking his Stetson from his head with a swashbuckling flourish, he waved it high.

The crowd went crazy.

Meg's heart pounded so hard that watching became actually painful. She'd never felt crowd excitement like this before, not even at the rodeos in Cheyenne and Denver. For the first time, she could understand why so many women responded to the cowboy charisma as instinctively as lemmings jump into the sea.

Jesse was magnificent. Since the horse offered no real challenge to his skill, Meg realized he'd decided to simply give the people what they wanted—a show. When the bucking tapered off, Jesse shifted the animal into a gallop. Racing from one end of the arena to the other, he reined up short and his mount stopped on the proverbial dime. He soon had the animal jumping right and left and practically running backward—in short, working like a seasoned cow pony.

With a final flourish of his hat, Jesse rode off to thunderous applause. He pulled the sorrel up in front of Meg, looking at her with a challenging light in his gray eyes. Excitement and tension radiated from his body and she felt a physical jolt. Like the knights of old, he seemed to be looking at her for some sign of favor.

Impulsively, she reached for the royal blue ribbon tied in a bow around the waist of her sundress. With a quick tug, the ribbon came undone. Leaning forward, she stretched out her arm with the ribbon fluttering from her fingers.

"You were wonderful!" she cried. In the general tumult, she couldn't be sure if he heard her or not. "I don't know what would have happened if you hadn't been there."

Jesse stood up in the stirrups and stretched to take the ribbon from her hand. She thought she heard him say, "I'll always be there." Then he hauled the sorrel around and galloped to the center of the arena, his arm aloft so that Meg's ribbon streamed out behind him.

The noisy approval of the crowd sounded out of proportion to its modest size. And it was all for Jesse, she realized with pride.

This time when he returned, he stepped out of the saddle and tossed the reins over the horse's head. The animal stood with heaving sides, but its eyes still rolled white in their sockets. Meg climbed down from the fence, just as a burly red-faced man with a handlebar mustache rushed up. The newcomer made a grab for the horse's reins.

Jesse stepped between man and animal, his eyes narrowing. "Billy Vaughn, if you let that kid of yours loose with this horse again before he's big enough and smart enough to ride him, I personally am going to clean your plow. Somebody coulda got killed here."

"Aw, J.J." The man hunched his shoulders miserably. "I know it. I feel awful about the whole thing. I'm sellin' that horse, yes-siree-bob, that horse is *gone.*"

The man stuck out his hand, and it looked as if he held his breath waiting to see what response he'd get. "I'd sell the kid if I could find anybody dumb enough to take him," he added hopefully.

Jesse let out his breath in a great sigh. "Aw, hell," he said, sounding disgusted. "I don't want the kid, but I'll take the horse. Haul him on out to my place tomorrow and bring me a bill of sale—I'll write you a check."

Billy's eyes lit up and his mustache lifted above a huge grin. "When it comes to horse tradin', you Taggarts beat all," he declared, slapping his hand against one thigh. "This is a fine animal, fine—a little spirited, but you're the ol' boy can handle him! You won't be sorry, J.J., no-siree-bob."

"I'm already sorry, Billy, but the deal's done." The two men shook hands. Only then did Jesse relinquish the reins. With a final expression of thanks, Billy led the now docile horse from the field.

"Meg." Jesse turned toward her and held out his hand.

Something had inexplicably changed between them and she realized he knew it, too. Danger had somehow stripped away the protective layers, revealing the true emotions long buried beneath manufactured defenses. She lifted her hand to place it in his—

"Nice ridin', cowboy!" Joe Bob thrust his bulk between them, ham-fisted hands slamming down on Jesse's shoulders with rough affection.

Shunted aside, Meg watched with growing exasperation. She felt ignored and left out. Jesse gave her an anxious tight-lipped glance and she shrugged, as if it didn't matter.

But it did.

Suzi trailed behind Joe Bob. When the big man stepped aside, she slipped past him and threw her arms around Jesse's neck.

"Ohhhhh—you're wonderful! I just love a man who takes control!" She lunged at him but he ducked aside and her kiss slid off his jaw, leaving a bright smear of lipstick on the collar of his pale blue shirt.

Laughing, she released him. "Good thing your wife's here," she said flirtatiously, slanting a quick glance at Meg. "Otherwise you might have some trouble explaining that lipstick on your collar."

Who told her? Meg's stomach lurched and she stared at Jesse, her mouth suddenly dry. He looked equally startled. But not Joe Bob—Meg thought she surprised a sly expression on his face before he realized she was looking at him and assumed an air of innocence.

She needed to talk to Jesse now, but she found she literally had to stand in line as he was swallowed up by admirers. Nor could she blame the townspeople; he had been theirs before he was hers, if he ever *had* been hers. Donna gave him a hug; even little Shane stammered his thanks.

At last the Hell's Bells Community Band began to play. Slowly the crowd shifted its attention to the bandstand for the speechifyin', as one old codger put it. Suddenly Jesse and Meg were alone, as alone as they could be in the middle of a community Fourth of July celebration.

He opened his arms and she walked into them. It was the most right thing that could have happened, for it told her that, after all was said and done, she was the one he wanted beside him. Sighing, she rested her cheek against his chest, her arms slipping around his lean waist with frightening ease.

"You took an awful chance," she whispered. "Not later, when you rode that crazy horse, but when you jumped in front of him that way...."

"I saw those kids coming around the corner and I thought of Randy," he said in a low voice. "And I saw you. That jughead would've run right over you. Lord, Meggie! If anything had happened to you—"

She felt his kiss on the top of her head and tightened her arms around him, pressing her breasts against his solid strength. A sense of security stole over her and she heard herself saying words that surprised her as much as they must have surprised him. "Jesse, when that blond bombshell, Suzi, tried to kiss you and got lipstick on your collar, is that... is that how it happened the other time?"

She felt the groan rumble through his broad chest. He didn't have to ask which other time.

"Yep," he said at last. "Pretty much."

She clenched her fingers in his shirt. "Then why wouldn't you explain? *Why,* Jesse?"

"Aw, honey." His voice sounded heavy with frustration. "What good are explanations? You look at the evidence, consider the circumstances and decide what the hell it means. Now if you'd found a lady's unmentionables in my pocket, that would have been a whole different story. I could understand something like that making you mad. But lipstick..."

When he put it like that.... "Jesse," she whispered, "if you'd said all this in the first place, the last five years might have been entirely different."

"Meggie—" his arm tightened convulsively around her "—let's go home."

Not yet! She knew what he was suggesting, but she wasn't ready to make that commitment. She needed to adjust to what was happening between them. She placed her palms flat against his chest. "You're going too fast," she said breathlessly. "There'll be fireworks later—we don't want to miss them."

He caught her hands in both of his and lifted them to his lips. His steady gaze held hers. "Not a chance," he said with absolute certainty.

CHAPTER FIVE

JESSE BROUGHT Meg barbecue, great slabs of genuine mesquite-cooked Texas brisket, served up with corn on the cob and sweet red slices of vine-ripened tomatoes. They ate at the top of the grandstand while kids took over the arena for the three-legged race, the potato race, the egg toss...

Meg thought she'd never laughed so hard or had so much fun in her life. All the barriers she'd erected to protect herself from her own feelings seemed to have tumbled like the walls of Jericho. She felt giddy with joy and drunk with... anticipation.

"Lemonade?" Jesse asked.

She jerked away from such disturbing thoughts and smiled her thanks. She drank thirstily, the liquid tart and cool on her tongue. "What happens next?" she asked, referring to the events of the celebration.

A slow smile transformed his lean face. "What do you want to happen next?" he asked in a voice at once rough and tender.

She gulped. She had to clear her throat to get out a single word: "F-fireworks?"

He laughed. "I like a woman with a one-track mind," he teased. "The lady wants fireworks, fireworks she shall have."

But not until dark, a couple of hours away. There was plenty of time to wander hand in hand through the picnic area. Jesse had a greeting for most everyone, and he and Meg paused frequently to exchange small talk with the locals. For the first time, she actually began to feel as if she belonged in his world.

At the game booth sponsored by the local men's service club, the Hell's Bellians, Jesse won an ugly stuffed bear by tossing horseshoes. He handed the prize to Meg with a flourish.

"Is there no end to your talents?" she teased, clasping the bear to her bosom as if it were the loveliest of God's creatures.

"No," he said seriously, but his eyes gleamed with challenge. "No end whatsoever."

As they neared the chili booth, the chef himself waved them over. "Tell these folks," Joe Bob ordered, indicating the middle-aged couple standing at the counter. "Do I make the best chili in the world or what?"

"Or what," Meg said promptly, although Joe Bob had ignored her and spoken directly to Jesse. She was rewarded with a hostile glance.

Jesse considered more carefully. Finally he said, "I can't speak for the world but I can honestly state that in Hell's Bells, Texas, Joe Bob's chili is in a class all by itself."

Joe Bob beamed. "See," he said triumphantly. "I told you so. Here, take a bite." He dug around with a spoon in a paper cup.

"Not me," the man said, his accent clearly indicating he hailed from some point north of the Mason-Dixon Line. "Uh-uh, no way. Come on, Dorothy, I want another beer."

The woman shook her head. "You go on, Larry. I think I may work up the nerve to try some of this genuine Texas chili."

"Your funeral," Larry said.

Added Joe Bob, sotto voce, to Jesse, "He got that right."

Dorothy keyed in on the exchange. "I'm sorry, were you speaking to me?"

"Just invitin' my friends here to watch fireworks with me later," Joe Bob lied blithely. "Now about this chili..."

Dorothy looked doubtful. "I've never eaten rattlesnake," she admitted, watching with reluctant fascination as Joe Bob stirred the mixture in the cup.

"Few people have, darlin', few people have. That's what makes my chili so special—that and the tomatas."

Dorothy frowned. "Is it hot? I wouldn't want to destroy my taste buds or anything."

Joe Bob scoffed. "Hot? Only from the fire. Ask anybody, they'll tell you." He appealed to Jesse. "Tell this pore foreign lady, J.J."

Meg shifted uncomfortably and Jesse's hand closed viselike around hers. His face was the picture of innocence.

"It's hot from the fire, all right," Jesse announced. "That's definite."

Both Joe Bob and Dorothy seemed satisfied with that answer and resumed their discussion with some spirit. Meg, however, was *not* satisfied.

Turning her back to the booth, she gestured Jesse to lean closer. "Remember what you said earlier about a mouth transplant? What have you got against that lady, Jesse?"

He laughed. "Not a thing. Joe Bob's just havin' a little fun."

"I don't think practical jokes are fun, especially not the kind he plays. That woman probably *will* ruin her taste buds. At the very least, it's going to ruin her Fourth of July."

Jesse shrugged. "Hey, it's none of my business. I didn't lie—that stuff *is* hot from the fire. Of course, it's also hot from a gallon or two of fresh chili peppers, but nobody asked about that." He tugged at her hand. "Let's go find a spot to watch fireworks."

"Well . . ."

Meg hesitated, glancing over her shoulder. Dorothy held the cup in one hand and a spoon in the other—not the small plastic spoon but a big wooden job heaped with Joe Bob's chili.

"That's it," Joe Bob cajoled, voice as soothing as if he spoke to a skittish mare. "Best way to savor the bo-kay garn-ee is with one larrupin' big mouthful."

Like a mongoose staring at a snake, Dorothy slowly leaned close to the spoon. Meg held her breath and tried mental telepathy. *Don't do it, Dorothy!*

Dorothy opened her mouth and Meg screamed, "No!"

The spoon clattered from the woman's grip, splattering chili all over the counter. Her shocked glance swung to Meg.

A wave of red suffused Joe Bob's face. "Dad-burn it, Maggie, you are the gol-dangdest, contrariest woman." He banged one big fist down on the countertop for emphasis.

Meg gasped and took a hasty step backward. She hadn't meant to get involved; her husband's best friend already disliked her enough and now he'd probably hate her. Was Jesse angry? She risked a glance over her shoulder.

Jesse was laughing! He slipped his arms around her in a protective manner and laughed and laughed and laughed. "You had her going, Joe Bob," he gasped.

"Well, I never!" Dorothy slammed down the cup. "If you can't trust a cowboy, who can you trust?" She whirled away, took two steps, stopped and looked at Meg. "Thank you," she said with dignity. "You've at least partially restored my faith in the basic decency of Texans." She darted a furious glance at Joe Bob. "Partially!"

Meg also looked at Joe Bob, and caught him glaring at her. She shivered. She knew she'd done the right thing, but perhaps she'd done it in the wrong way.

At the very least, any lingering doubts about Joe Bob's enmity toward her had been swept away.

THE HELL'S BELLS Community Band wasn't exactly the Boston Pops, and the display of fireworks over the picnic grounds didn't rival the show put on each year over Boston Harbor. Still, Meg had never enjoyed an Independence Day celebration more.

Sitting on the grass with her back against the trunk of a tree, she looked down at Jesse, illuminated by the rocket's red glare. He lay with his head on her lap, his hat tumbling aside when she slid her fingers through his hair. He looked comfortable and at ease—but she knew he wasn't, any more than she was. His tension transmitted itself clearly to her through every point where their bodies touched. He must feel her own tension with equal clarity.

One splendid *boom!* after another rent the air. Shower after shower of brilliant sparks of light cascaded through the dark sultry skies. All the "Oohs!" and "Ahhs!" reached a crescendo with the final magnificent explosion blossoming into an American flag flanked by pinwheels and fountains and the Lone Star of Texas. Spontaneous applause burst from the observers.

The last ember faded from the sky. For a moment the darkness seemed total, and then somewhere, somebody threw a switch. Electric light flooded the area. The crowd began to stir, rise, move toward the exit.

Meg sat quietly, all her attention centered on Jesse as he lay looking up at her with dark impenetrable eyes.

"Ready to go home, Meg?"

A pulse leapt in her throat. It was her choice. Impulsively, she brushed light fingertips across his lips. He went rigid but his gaze never wavered.

And she heard herself saying, "Yes. I'm ready, Jesse. Yes."

BUT WAS SHE?

Riding beside him in the cab of the pickup truck through the torrid Texas night, Meg began to wonder. *Yes,* he was the most exciting man she'd ever met; *yes,* she was wildly attracted to him; *yes,* it was hell living under the same roof with him without letting herself love him.

But their differences were too great. Jesse was a man's man, living out the male fantasy of the cowboy—a self-sufficient loner pursued by many women. That's what he'd always been, and *no,* she didn't believe he'd changed; *no,* she didn't believe he'd ever let one woman become indispensable to him; and *no,* she wasn't willing to settle for anything less.

She was East and he was West; he was spontaneous and she was deliberate; he ignored public opinion and she lived by it.

The odds were too great! She was out of the truck almost before it pulled to a complete stop in front of the cabin and halfway up the steps before he caught her. When he did, he swung her into his arms, carried her to the front door and pushed it open with one well-aimed kick.

For a moment he stood on the threshold, breathing hard. Then he stepped inside and kicked the door closed behind him. "I've missed you," he said in a ragged voice.

It was darker inside than out. Surrounded by total blackness, she felt everything magnified a hundred times—his strong arms holding her so easily, his chest heaving beneath her cheek, the wild pounding of her own heart.

"Jesse..." She heard the panic and uncertainty in her voice. Bracing one hand against his chest, she leaned away from him.

He tightened his arms in response. "Don't. Don't say anything yet. We've got to get used to being together all over again. Wait..."

His voice soothed and coaxed, and she took some comfort when he lowered her legs and stood her on her own two feet. Only she didn't stand independently; his arm clamped around her waist to crush her against him. Nothing had ever felt so good. A tiny moan escaped her.

"Yes," he whispered. "Yes, that's right. We always had this, no matter how bad things got. You remember, too. I thought you didn't, but every time I touch you . . . I know."

He kissed her throat, her temple, her ear. His breath tickled and teased, and she found herself squirming, pressing against him, wanting more.

"Jesse," she gasped, her head falling back to expose her vulnerable throat to his questing lips. "I . . . I'm not sure we should be doing this!"

He pressed his mouth to the full slope of her breast above the sundress, his low laughter muffled. She bent before him like a reed caught in gale-force winds.

"It's inevitable," he murmured against her blooming flesh. "You're my wife, Meggie—how could I let you forget that for so long?"

He straightened and his lips found hers in another searing kiss. A kiss that fit exactly with what she felt—a desperation to wipe away all the hurt and deprivation of their time apart.

He picked her up in his arms and she clung to him when he carried her into the big bedroom where she'd lain awake through endless nights, dreamed dreams very much like this reality. He placed her on the wedding-ring-patterned quilt.

She wanted him, needed him, but the depth of her feelings frightened her. She knew he wanted her, too, but for how long? No words of love or commitment had passed his lips.

He looked down at her, illuminated by moonlight streaming through the window. "Fireworks," he said in a voice thick with passion. "A million Roman candles aren't enough to describe the way you make me feel."

That just about said it all, Meg acknowledged as she surrendered her final misgivings.

THEY SLEPT; they awoke in darkness, she didn't know how much later. All she knew was that when he touched her that way, her senses leapt in instant response.

"Honey, we have to talk," she suggested breathlessly, her arms sliding around his neck.

"Later. Right now...we have to find out...what happens when I..."

Despite her best intentions, she gave herself up to the glory of his mouth, his hands, his strong sensual body and seductive voice. She surrendered because...because she loved him. Because maybe there was a chance for them, after all. Because he came to her with equal parts passion and tenderness, and her desperate heart chose to interpret the tenderness as love.

Much later, she tried again. "Jesse...about that talk...."

He yawned and molded her more tightly against his side. "Do we have to?"

She laughed at the plaintive note in his voice. "Yes, we have to." She relented slightly. "But not right now. How about first thing in the morning?"

"Sure." He sounded relieved. And sleepy. "First thing in the morning. If you insist."

"I insist. Promise?"

Another yawn. "Sure. I promise."

"Good, because this is important." Satisfied with his murmur of acquiescence, she went on, "Not that I'm looking forward to it. It's just that I'm completely unprepared for...this. Us like this, I mean. Maybe you considered it inevitable that we'd...get together. I didn't. But it's happened, and there's no way we can go back. Now we have to decide what to do about it. Because Jesse, I won't be an occasional diversion to you—no way!''

She waited tensely for some response. And waited.

"Jesse?"

A soft sigh greeted her and he curled his body more closely around hers. Jesse was sound asleep. Meg wondered if he'd heard a single word.

SHE OPENED HER EYES to a brand-new world. For a moment she lay perfectly still, letting the events of the past twenty-four hours rush over her.

Letting the events of the last eight hours carry her away.... She realized she was smiling and that made her laugh out loud at her own transparency.

"Jesse!"

She bounced around in an empty bed, disappointed but not surprised to find he wasn't beside her. He'd always been an early riser, while she never missed a chance to sleep in. Now fully awake, she noticed the sounds of activity in the kitchen and supposed he was preparing breakfast, or at least making coffee.

Still smiling, she stretched luxuriously and lay back in the bed, pulling the sheet up to her chin. In a few minutes she would face him and confess—confess to loving him still.

She'd never stopped loving him and never would; she supposed she'd always known that on some level. But she'd either be treated with the respect she deserved as a woman and as a wife or she'd walk away. She'd done it before and she could do it again if necessary.

Only of course now it wasn't necessary. Last night had proven that to her. Last night had been ... A slow, secret smile curved her lips. What had happened between them was love, pure and simple.

When he came in to wake her, what would she say to him? Should she make a bold declaration or should she wait for him to speak first? Her smile grew wry; in all likelihood she'd wait forever for him to speak first. Jesse didn't like to discuss his feelings; she supposed most men shared that aversion. Perhaps she should...

She heard the sound of an approaching vehicle and lay still for a moment, listening. The blast of a horn brought her onto her knees to peek between the curtains at the head of the bed.

Joe Bob—damn! Meg let the curtain drop and sat back on legs folded beneath her, frowning. When minutes passed and she neither heard him drive away nor enter the house, she rose to her knees again and raised just a corner of the curtain.

Jesse stood beside the driver's window of the pickup, listening intently, she judged from the tilt of his head. Joe Bob was talking a mile a minute, but Meg couldn't hear what he was saying. Whatever he was up to, she was sure it wouldn't work. Not this time.

She saw Jesse shake his head and glance toward the house. She could just imagine his saying, "Not now. Meg and I have some important things to discuss. I promised."

She'd be ready for that talk when Jesse came inside, she vowed. Quickly she showered and dressed. Coming out of the bathroom, she heard Joe Bob gun his engine as if about to leave.

Poor old Joe Bob, she thought, trying to be gracious in victory. She parted the curtains, just in time to see the pickup turn around. Joe Bob glanced toward the window and his glance locked with Meg's; he flipped her an obscene gesture and passed out of sight.

Then she saw Jesse, sitting in the passenger seat. He never even looked back.

FIRST SHE WENT CRAZY.

Her thrifty New England heritage wouldn't allow her to do what she wanted to do—burn the cabin to the ground and her humiliation along with it—so instead she went into a cleaning frenzy. Within a half hour her hands were raw from the strong ammonia solution in her bucket and her eyes were red from the fumes of the oven cleaner. Or so she told herself.

She scrubbed the bathtub so hard she damaged the caulking; she broke a fingernail scouring the kitchen sink; the dust from the throw rugs flew into her eyes and mouth and hair, and still Jesse didn't return.

Not until almost noon.

Meg, sitting at the table with her head cradled in her arms, heard the pickup outside. He walked into the cabin, and she looked up wearily. She intended to be calm and reasonable. She'd tried hard to convince herself she could afford to be, since he was entirely at fault.

But when she saw his worried expression and realized he knew perfectly well that she'd be upset, all her good intentions flew right out the window. "You despicable, deceitful...cowboy!" she cried with heartfelt sincerity.

He flinched as if she'd landed an uppercut. "Now hang on a minute before you fly off the handle—"

"A minute? I've waited hours!" She rose to stand with arms braced on the tabletop. "You do remember we were supposed to talk first thing this morning?"

"Sure I remember." His face took on that familiar stubborn expression.

"Well?"

"Well, what?"

"I don't hear any explanations!" She shoved raw fingers through her short curls and tried to keep her lips from trembling. "Lord, I should have known! Why do I keep letting you do this to me?"

"Just a damned minute!" An answering anger suffused Jesse's chiseled features. "'First thing in the morning' for me was about six-fifteen. I was here—where were you?"

"You know where I was—where you left me!"

"Well, I'm here now. What's so all-fired important, anyway?"

They were shouting at each other; after that incredible night together, they were further apart at this moment than they'd ever been, Meg realized. Obviously what she'd mistaken for love had, indeed, been nothing more than sex—okay, great sex. But that still wasn't enough.

She winced at that realization. "Only one thing is important now—Randy," she cried, her voice rising with each word. "That's all I have to talk to you about, now or ever!"

"You don't mean that." He stalked toward her and she retreated, putting the table between them. "After last night—"

"Last night was a mistake—the biggest mistake I ever made in my life! Please spare me the humiliation of referring to it ever again."

It broke her heart to say those words, and he looked stunned to hear them. She flounced past him, but he reached out and grabbed her arm, stopping her in her tracks.

"Now *I'm* the one saying we have to talk," he announced grimly.

Even in her current state of disillusionment, her heart leapt at his touch. She looked down at his hand on her arm. "Yes," she agreed, her voice flat. "We have to talk—about Randy. But first, I want you to get your hand off me and I don't *ever* want you to touch me again."

He looked as if she'd slapped him, but he released her. "You're sure that's how you want it?"

"Oh, yes, I'm very sure."

He shrugged and turned away, his back rigid.

"And Jesse?"

He paused without turning around.

"I'll give this one more week for Randy's sake and then I'm going home. I've got better things to do with my time than play games with you."

For a moment she thought he wouldn't even respond. Then he said in a voice that sent prickles down her spine, "Games, huh. You sure as hell got that right."

"HE'S NOT GOING to that sissy school and that's final!"

"It's one of the finest schools in the country, if not the world. He'll learn—"

"Why do you want to get rid of him? I always thought you loved him, but this makes me wonder if—"

"How dare you! This is a *day* school, right there in Boston! He'll be home every night, and every weekend. He'll—"

"Spend all his time on buses? No way!"

"Harris will drive him. Harris will pick him up. For heaven's sake, Jesse—"

"Grandpa's chauffeur? I get it. This is a school for snobs as well as sissies, right? He's not going to some sissy school for snobs and that's final!"

"No, you can't have him for Christmas and that's final."

"Why the hell not? He doesn't have any fun in Boston with the decorator trees and caroling around the wassail bowl or whatever the hell you aristocrats do."

"Temper, temper!"

"Hey, my folks didn't come over on the *Mayflower*. I'm just a down-home hell-raiser. Of course, Taggarts did fight at the Alamo."

"At the Alamo and at the drop of a hat—I know. You Texans are all alike. You consider everything east of the Mississippi too crowded and cramped for human habitation, but all that proves to me is that you're the real snob! At least Boston is civilized—"

"You're sayin' Texas isn't? Watch it, Margaret, you're about to shoot yourself in the foot."

AND SO IT WENT for the first two days of Jesse's week of grace—forty-eight hours of hell. By the third day, she'd had enough.

She'd hit the end of her rope. Otherwise, she'd never have gone to the Hell's Bells Low Life Saloon alone.

CHAPTER SIX

MEG DIDN'T *plan* to go to a saloon, alone or otherwise. It just happened. One minute she was walking to her car from the Texas Rose Drugs and Sundries store and the next she was pushing through the batwing doors of the saloon and plopping herself down on a stool at the ornate bar.

The bartender, a paunchy man with a handlebar mustache who looked vaguely familiar, glanced up from the counter he was polishing.

"White zinfandel, please," Meg announced, depositing her package of sunscreen lotion and dental floss on the bar. "I skipped lunch—do you serve food?"

The bartender seemed nonplussed. "After six," he said. "How 'bout chablis? We don't serve pink wine that lies about itself."

"Chablis will be fine."

"We got pork rinds and pigs' feet," the barkeep said helpfully, unscrewing the cap on the wine bottle. He looked around for an appropriate glass, spotted a couple on the back of the shelf and pulled one out. "Got a bunch of dudes comin' in later for happy hour and we'll put out some eats then—boiled eggs, sausage, that kinda thing."

Meg could see the dust on the wineglass from where she sat. He rinsed and polished it with a bar towel, then poured the wine.

He set the glass before her. "Sure you want this on a empty stomach, Miz Taggart?"

"You're right. It is a bad idea." She sighed. "I'll take some of those pork rinds, I guess. It ... it's not really the wine I came in for, anyway, it's the atmosphere." *And to delay returning to the cabin.*

"Yeah," he agreed. "Dudes always like it."

She could see why. It was exactly what a Wild West saloon should be, from the ornate Victorian bar to the painting of a plump naked lady on the wall. At the moment the saloon was nearly empty. A middle-aged couple, dressed like tourists, sat talking at a table in the corner. An older man who looked like a local stood at the far end of the bar, nursing a beer.

The bartender pulled a cellophane bag off a clip and sent it sliding down the mahogany to her. She smiled her thanks. "Have we met?" she asked. "You know my name and I'm afraid I don't ... ?"

"No reason you should. I'm Billy Vaughn. The young hellion who nearly got hisself killed at the Fourth of July celebration was my boy, Little Billy." He scowled.

Meg felt her cheeks flush. "Jesse was a bit outspoken in his criticism," she murmured. "I'm sorry if he offended you."

Billy threw back his head and stared at her. "Hell, I weren't offended! I just thank my lucky stars J.J. was there. I seen him grow from boy to man and he's a good one, all right." His brows lowered in a frown. "But I don't reckon he'd be any too pleased to know his wife's suckin' up the sauce in the middle of the afternoon.''

Before she could overcome her astonishment, Billy turned away. *Let him think what he wants,* she decided. One glass of wine scarcely constituted ''suckin' up the sauce.'' She'd told him the truth; she was here for the atmosphere, not the alcohol. The Hell's Bells Low Life Saloon was cool and quiet, and the town outside was as hot as its namesake.

Besides, she'd never been here with Jesse, so it held no memories for her. That, in itself, was a big plus. She lifted her glass to take the first sip.

''Meg!''

Startled, Meg sloshed wine over the rim of her glass. Glancing toward the door, she saw Laurel Anderson hurrying toward her. ''Hi, Laurel,'' she said, surprised but pleased to see a familiar face. ''Fancy meeting you here.''

Laurel slid onto the stool next to Meg's. Only half the length of the long bar was fronted by stools; the rest had only a foot rail, more in keeping with the spirit of the past. ''You okay, honey?'' she asked anxiously.

It dawned on Meg that Laurel's appearance was no accident. She frowned. ''Of course I'm okay. Is that why you're here, to check up on me?''

Laurel looked uncomfortable. ''Well, sort of,'' she admitted. ''When Donna come into the store and told me she saw you headin' in here—''

''Donna!''

''She likes you, Meg. She told me you were ready to stand up to that runaway horse to protect Shane and the other kids, which makes you okay in her book. Mine, too.''

She caught Billy's attention and ordered a beer before continuing. "Since I'm here and can plainly see you're fine, might as well have a cold one before I go back to work," she explained cheerfully. "So how's it going? Sure was nice to see you and J.J. so cozy on the Fourth."

Meg considered her options. She longed to confide her inability to understand her husband. And who better to talk to than Laurel, who'd known Jesse all his life? "To tell you the truth, Laurel—"

"Billy, Joe Bob says tell you he's on the way with eleven thirsty drugstore cowboys!"

Suzi Sherman paused just inside the swinging doors as if to give everyone a chance to admire her cowgirl chic—which looked as if it might have been painted on. Long platinum-blond hair flowed from beneath a white Stetson; her stretch jeans and boots were also white. A sheer, black-lace T-shirt completed her ensemble, with nothing whatsoever beneath it except Suzi herself. That her bountiful breasts were unfettered was readily apparent to the most casual observer.

Laurel groaned and spoke out of the corner of her mouth. "Tacky, tacky, tacky. There goes the neighborhood, honey."

Meg stifled laughter. "Maybe she won't notice us," she suggested hopefully.

Faint hope soon dashed.

"Meg! How...nice!" Suzi swayed toward the bar. "I'll have vodka on the rocks, Billy. Hello, Laurel. Surprised to find you here in the middle of the day. But really, Meg, I never expected to see *you* here at all. What a nice surprise—Joe Bob didn't say anything about you meeting us."

Meg pushed her untouched wine aside and picked up her package. "I'm not meeting anybody. I stopped here on an impulse—" *which I deeply regret* "—and now I'm leaving."

"At least wait until I finish my beer!" Laurel lifted her mug and took a deep swallow.

Suzi picked up the glass Billy set before her. "If she's got to go, she's got to go," she said in an indifferent tone. "Maybe another time, Meg."

"Maybe." Meg slid off her stool. She didn't want to be here when Joe Bob walked in, that was for sure. Wouldn't he just love to be the one to tell Jesse his wife was into booze in the afternoon?

Actually, Meg now admitted this hadn't been a very good idea. There was no anonymity to be had for a Taggart in this town, even a Taggart-by-marriage. The word had spread like wildfire; before the batwing doors swung shut behind her, half the town apparently knew that Meg Taggart was in the Hell's Bells Low Life Saloon.

Not that she cared if Jesse found out, she reminded herself defiantly. What she did was no longer any concern of his, as long as she remained within the bounds of propriety. But out of deference to his celebrity status, she wouldn't go out of her way to embarrass or annoy him—or herself, for that matter. Coming face-to-face in a bar with his best friend, even a skunk like Joe Bob, was to be avoided at all costs.

So Meg clutched her package and her purse, feeling an overwhelming desire to flee. "Nice seeing you both," she murmured, digging around for money to pay for her drink. "How much...?"

Noise from outside arrested her attention and she glanced up, distracted, dreading but resigned to seeing Joe Bob.

That, at least, she was spared. For leading the noisy happy group into the Hell's Bells Low Life Saloon was Jesse James Taggart.

THERE WAS PLENTY of subtext to their conversation, Meg realized. She was sure Jesse did, too.

"Why, hello, honey. I didn't know you were coming into town today." *What the hell are you doing sitting in a saloon drinking in the middle of the day?*

"I needed a few things. I left shortly after you did." *And if you ever hung around, you'd know these things. You're always out with your buddies.*

"Ol' Billy take good care of you?" *Besides storin' up anecdotes about J. J. Taggart's Yankee wife to regale the regulars with, of course.*

"Oh, yes. And so did Laurel and Suzi." *Suzi knew where you were and I didn't have a clue. How do you think that makes me feel?*

Just about like I feel findin' you in here. "Can I get you something to eat?"

Don't be obvious—I'm not drunk! This is my first glass of wine and I haven't even tasted it yet. "I had a lovely bag of pork rinds but didn't get a chance to enjoy them."

"Billy's putting out the happy hour spread for Joe Bob's people now. I'm sure I can find something more to your liking than pork rinds." *But no bird's nest soup or fricasseed gnats' knees, I'm afraid.*

"Don't bother. I was just leaving." *Let me out of here before...*

Jesse leaned across the table where they'd retreated for some privacy. He covered her hand with his, the expression on his face turning vulnerable.

"Don't." He said the single word as if he didn't want to but couldn't help himself. "Stay. I only agreed to loan ol' Joe Bob a hand wranglin' dudes because you wouldn't give me the time of day. At least we're talking now. Sort of."

Meg looked down at their hands on top of the table. She had automatically turned her palm toward his and their fingers were entwined.

He was right; the last couple of days had been miserable. If she stayed a few minutes, what could be the harm? They were surrounded by people; better here than alone at the cabin.

She let out the breath she'd unconsciously been holding. "All right," she agreed stiffly. "I'll stay for a little while. And I'd love something to eat. Thank you for offering."

His smile lit up his face—and the entire room.

JESSE NEVER LEFT her side, not even when Joe Bob tried to entice him into spinning a few yarns for the tenderfoot audience. Laurel finished her beer and went back to work, leaving Jesse and Meg alone in the crowd.

By mutual but unspoken consent, they avoided topics guaranteed to strike sparks. They talked about the weather, the lack of rainfall, the salad Meg made for dinner the night before. They didn't talk about the tension, their sleeping arrangements or their son.

When somebody shoved coins in the jukebox, Jesse held out his hand. "Come dance with me, darlin'," he invited.

Meg reached for his hand, then pulled back. She stared at him, wide-eyed, trying to fathom his motives. Movement distracted her; Suzi descended upon them, syrupy voice inquiring, "You don't mind me borrowing your handsome husband for just one little dance, do you, Meg?"

Meg minded very much. "Sorry," she said, taking Jesse's hand. He gave her the long slow smile she loved and led her onto the small dance floor at the back of the room. He didn't once look Suzi's way.

Meg had never danced with anyone else the way she'd always danced with Jesse, right from that very first time in Aspen. It wasn't that he was a brilliant or fancy dancer, it was just that everything fit so well. Her rhythm matched his; her feet understood his and moved accordingly. With natural grace, he led her effortlessly; she followed the same way.

There was a physical communication between them when they danced, a communication that transcended words. Lost in the moment, she felt the angry tension drain away, and that other, more dangerous tension replace it.

"Change partners! C'mon, now, change partners!"

Meg's eyes flew open; she hadn't even realized she was dancing with them closed, her cheek pressed against Jesse's shoulder. Joe Bob's raucous words shattered the moment. Before she could object, he dragged her from Jesse's embrace and into his own. Suzi was right there to slide her arms around Jesse's neck.

Meg caught a glimpse of Jesse's scowl before Joe Bob crushed her in a bear hug that threatened to break her in two. He danced her quickly away to the other side of the floor, holding her in a death grip.

"I can't breathe!"

She finally got her palms against his chest and gave him a shove. He hung on, darting a quick glance back over his shoulder. Meg's gaze followed his.

She saw Suzi, draped all over Jesse, a dreamy expression on her overly made-up face. Jesse appeared to be dancing with wary caution—but how wary could he be, with a beautiful blonde pressing herself against him that way?

"I should have known," Meg muttered.

"Known what, darlin'?" Joe Bob dragged her reluctant body through several spins and dips.

Known what a louse you are, she thought. "Known you'd show up today," she improvised.

"Sure did surprise your old man to find you here," Joe Bob said cheerfully.

"Don't call him that. Jesse's my husband, not my old man."

"Sorry, Maggie. Whatever you call him, you two got a real curious marriage goin'. You coulda knocked him over with a feather when he saw you boozin' it up in the shank of the day."

"Yes, well, I like to keep him off balance." No point in trying to reason with this clown, she told herself.

"That you do, Maggie m'love, that you do." The music ended but he didn't let her go immediately. "I hear yawl'll be headin' back to Boston soon."

Meg stiffened. *Has Jesse been talking to Joe Bob about our personal problems?* "Probably," she said with icy caution. "Why do you ask?"

He shrugged, but his eyes looked even more shrewd than usual. "I'm havin' a big barbecue at the ranch Saturday night. I'd be mighty proud to have you come."

"You've got to be joking."

"If you say so. J.J.'s promised to be there, but—"

"He has?" Stung to the quick, she yanked free. On her last night at the cabin, Jesse had made plans to go out alone? That certainly told her where she rated.

Joe Bob cast a knowing look at Jesse, deep in conversation with the blond bombshell. "Hey, lady, J.J. was my friend before he ever knew you was alive, and he'll be my friend long after you're—" He stopped as if aware he'd almost gone too far. "Look, yawl don't want to come to my party, fine. Just don't say I didn't ask you."

He tried to steer her off the dance floor but she held back. "What are you up to?" she wondered aloud. "I know you're still angry because I ruined your chili-joke on the Fourth of July—"

"Now why would I still be mad about a little ol' thing like that?"

"You shouldn't be. You got even for that when you showed up at the crack of dawn the next day and kidnapped Jesse."

"Why, I never!" Joe Bob looked insulted that she could suggest such a thing. "That horse woulda died sure's the lord made little green apples if Jesse hadn't helped me drag him outta—"

He stopped abruptly and glared at her. Despite herself, Meg smiled. So Jesse had been helping Joe Bob with a horse. Then why the blazes didn't he say so?

Joe Bob's mouth curled down. "Didn't know that, did you?"

"No."

"*Now* I owe you one."

WHEN JOE BOB loaded his dudes into the bus for the ride back to the ranch, Jesse declined to join them.

"I'll go home with Meg," he said, although he hadn't cleared that plan with her. "I'll come by tomorrow for my horse."

Joe Bob's disappointment was clear, but there wasn't much he could say without looking like a petulant kid. Suzi could, however.

"I'll see you at the barbecue Saturday night," she declared softly.

Jesse shrugged.

Suzi half turned, taking a deep breath that caused her breasts to thrust out boldly beneath the black stretch lace. "I won't forget what you said."

Meg's hackles rose as she watched Suzi's swing-hipped walk through the batwing doors. This kind of thing always made her crazy. Jesse should know a comment like that needed an explanation, but would he offer one?

Would she demand one?

Would she ask nicely for one? Beg for one?

Jesse sighed. "You've got that look on your face again."

"What look?" she asked stiffly.

"That he's-gonna-pay-for-this look." He pushed back his chair and stood up. "I'm ready to pay—for dinner. Let's go grab some grub at the Alamo Steak House."

The alternative, as she saw it, was to return together to the cabin. Once there, they'd either fight—

an unpleasant possibility—or *not* fight—a dangerous possibility.

All in all, the Alamo Steak House sounded fine.

THE WAITRESS cleared the table and poured coffee. Meg sighed and gave Jesse a rueful smile. "I ate too much," she admitted, "but it was wonderful."

"They do know how to treat a steak here," he agreed. He added a smidgen of sugar to his cup and stirred, not looking at her. "I . . . was a little surprised to find you in Billy's saloon earlier."

"Oh, for heaven's sake!" Meg leaned back in her chair, disgusted. "I wasn't overindulging in midday, if that's what worries you. As far as surprises go, I had no idea you were helping Joe Bob baby-sit his dudes until you walked in."

He frowned. "Don't jump on your high horse. I wanted to be the one to take you to Billy's, that's all. I figured it was the kind of place you'd like, with all that old stuff and the Wild West atmosphere. It's not as elaborate as the restorations in Showdown and a few other places, but it's got a certain charm."

"Oh." Somewhat mollified, she fiddled with her coffee cup. "I went in on an impulse. I guess I..." She gave him an oblique glance. "I wasn't eager to go back to the cabin. I don't know about you, but the strain is getting to me."

"You got that right!" He shook his head woefully. "Meg, why do we do this to each other? You've got me in such a state that half the time I don't know if I'm coming or going."

She stared at him. "That's news to me. You certainly act as if you know what you're doing at all times—although you've never been inclined to share that information with me."

"Damn!" He gave her a ruffled glance. "Why the hell did you marry me in the first place if I'm so lacking in the finer qualities? Sometimes I think that cold-blooded legal-eagle brother of mine's more your type than I am!"

"I met you both at the same time and I chose you!"

"Yeah." He leaned forward intently. "Why is that, do you suppose?"

"You know why," she said in a strangled voice.

"I thought I did, but hell! I'm not sure of anything anymore." He slumped back in his chair, expression brooding. "Spell it out. Why did you marry me?"

"Because I took one look at you and realized love at first sight does exist." She blurted out the admission. "Good grief, Jesse, two weeks—what could we possibly know about each other in that time?" She clenched her trembling hands into fists in her lap. "This is all your fault," she accused. "You're the one who proposed—Boone tried to talk you out of it, as perhaps you've conveniently forgotten. I'm the one who should be asking why—and I am. Why did you do it, Jesse? Why did *you* marry *me?*"

He groaned and closed his eyes for a second as if remembering. "I thought I knew what physical attraction was and then I met you and realized I didn't know diddly. I wanted you so bad my teeth ached. I wanted you forever so I proposed. It was dumb. You were too young, too spoiled and too stubborn."

"I was twenty, and I sure wasn't looking for a husband." She stared down at the untouched coffee cooling in her cup. "Maybe I was a little spoiled, but when it comes to stubborn, I could take lessons from you."

"Maybe you did. If so, you're a hell of a fast learner."

"Something wrong with the coffee, J.J.?"

They both started at the unexpected intrusion of the waitress, hovering at Jesse's elbow with the coffeepot in her hand.

"It's fine. We've just been talking."

"Take your time, honey." She gave them a quick smile and moved away.

Dutifully Jesse picked up his cup and took a swallow. Then he returned to the conversation as if they'd never been interrupted. "I was no model of maturity at twenty-four, either. The thing is, I thought we'd both grow up, and we'd be together to help each other do it. Then when you left..."

Meg's throat closed and for a moment she couldn't speak. When she could, she whispered, "You know why I left."

"Yes, but for a long time I thought there had to be more to it. It was such a stupid little thing."

"Not to me. It was...the last straw."

"Don't you think I finally figured that out?" He looked thoroughly rattled. "I kept thinking you'd come to your senses and come home."

"And I kept thinking you'd come to your senses and come after me."

"I'll never crawl, Meggie. Not even for you."

Looking at the grim set of his face, she knew they'd reached an impasse yet again. "I never wanted or expected you to crawl," she said slowly. "I was disappointed you didn't care enough to make even a gesture toward reconciliation."

He looked astonished. "What did you call me showing up on your doorstep in Boston?"

"Considering that almost a year had passed and you asked for your son, not your wife, I called it a slap in the face."

He let out a harsh breath. "When you put it that way...maybe...I can see your point." He grimaced at such a concession. "In my own defense, I've got to remind you that I spent three months of that time in and out of the hospital."

She'd had no idea. Even now, years after the fact, she felt a chill pass through her when she heard it. "That's news to me," she said as calmly as she could manage. "What happened?"

He hunched his shoulders uncomfortably. "Horse threw me."

She arched her brows. "Threw you where?"

"Through a corral fence."

"You might have told me. If I'd known—"

"Hold it right there!" His eyes flashed and his lips thinned out in a displeased line. "I didn't want you back under those circumstances. Truth is, after you left, my...concentration sorta went to hell. I was getting pretty banged up there for a while."

"I'm sorry."

"Sympathy's my least-favorite thing."

"All right, then, I'm glad! I'm just disappointed that horse didn't knock some sense into you!"

Their glances locked—hers, furious, his, astonished. Then the silliness of it all seemed to wash over them simultaneously and Jesse began to laugh. After a surprised hesitation, Meg joined in.

Finally she sat back and dabbed at her eyes with a corner of her napkin. "I think we could argue about whether or not the moon's made of green cheese,'' she said ruefully.

He smiled. "It is, you know."

"Don't get me started." She dropped the napkin onto the table and in so doing, noticed the waitress hovering in the background. "Uh-oh, we're the last people here. I think they want to close up."

"Time to go home?"

His hopeful tone puzzled her. Where else would they go?

And then she realized that "home" to him meant a little more than just walking in the door....

SHE THOUGHT he must surely be asleep. Otherwise, she'd never have stepped foot outside her bedroom door. But it was a stifling-hot night, and the thought of a tall glass of juice or soda became too tempting to resist.

She moved quietly down the hall, the ruffle of her long cotton gown brushing her insteps. She'd spent the evening and most of the afternoon in air-conditioning. That always seemed to make the heat even more unbearable.

That, and the look in Jesse's eyes. She'd braced herself for some overture from him when they'd gotten back to the cabin, and was both relieved and confused when none was forthcoming. When she announced firmly that she was going to bed, he gave her a long probing look and told her he had similar plans.

And that was that.

She found the refrigerator by touch and opened the door. Light flooded the room. She pulled out a carton of orange juice, gave the door a push and turned toward the counter.

A dark figure loomed there. Meg's heart leapt and she let out a little cry of alarm. The carton of juice dropped from suddenly numb fingers.

"Hey, it's only me!"

Jesse's voice. Meg groaned and pressed one hand to the wildly throbbing pulse in her throat. He was around the counter in a flash and pulling her into his arms.

"You scared me!" she accused, achingly aware of his bare chest beneath her cheek and hands. Why was her heart still pounding like this?

"I'm sorry, baby." He slid one hand to the back of her head and tilted her face up. "You knew I'd be—"

The rest was lost in his kiss. With a groan, Meg stretched up and slid her arms around his neck. She felt suspended there in the darkness, spinning out of control with no point of reference except this man.

Wildly he kissed her mouth, her closed eyes, her cheeks, his every touch a promise. He kissed her until she swayed in his arms, weak with wanting. Then his kisses changed, became confident and tender. He stroked her sides with restless hands, then clutched the folds of her nightgown in his fists.

He lifted his head, his breathing raspy. "I've missed you. I was beginning to think you'd changed your mind."

"Ch-changed my mind?" She felt befuddled, drunk with sensation.

"About us." He caught her by the waist and lifted her hips against his. "About tonight."

"Tonight was..." She dragged in a trembling breath, trying to think. "It was...maybe a breakthrough but not...not a license for you to take advantage of me, Jesse!''

She felt him stiffen, felt him begin to pull back.

"What the hell are you talking about?"

Somewhere she had to find the strength to step away from him and out of the arousing circle of his arms. "I'm not going to sleep with you!" she cried. "What happened on the Fourth of July was...it was a mistake!" She pushed his arms aside and stepped back, gripping the kitchen counter for much-needed support.

He began to swear. She heard his footsteps in the dark and then harsh light flooded the room. He advanced on her, wearing only a pair of jeans. His chest rippled with muscle and his biceps bulged as he clenched his hands into fists.

He halted before her. "Are you saying you didn't know I'd be out here waiting for you?"

She pressed her fingers into the unyielding tile of the countertop, remembering the feel of warm smooth skin. "How on earth would I know such a thing? I was hot and thirsty—"

"You're hot and *bothered*, lady. Why not face it?"

She felt her cheeks sting with embarrassment and lifted her head a notch higher. "Because it's wrong."

"But we're married! How can it be wrong?"

She shook her head, fighting the prickle of tears behind her eyelids. "That's just a technicality. Maybe it's time we faced it. A piece of paper doesn't make a marriage. A marriage is commitment, and l-love."

He groaned. "Meggie, don't do this. You're my wife. I want—"

"I know what you want!" She pushed away from the counter and took two steps toward the hallway.

She clenched her hands together in front of her breast. "You'll have to find yourself another playmate to get it—which shouldn't be too hard. You already know where to look!"

She turned and fled down the hall, but not fast enough to escape his furious voice. "You got *that* right, babe. You sure as hell got that right!"

CHAPTER SEVEN

MEG STUMBLED across the bedroom in the dark, stubbing her toe on the bed frame. The pain sent tears sliding down her cheeks, tears she'd been fighting. Clutching her arms across her waist, she sat down in the rocking chair. A feeling of utter hopelessness washed over her.

She had as much as thrown him into the arms of another woman. What man would be strong enough to resist such a challenge?

The front door slammed. Jumping up, she ran to the window and pulled the curtains aside.

She saw Jesse, walking briskly through the silvery moonlight with long determined strides. Without a backward glance, he sprang into the cab of the pickup, started the engine and drove away.

Meg groaned and let the curtain drop back into place. Damn him! If he thought she'd sit up all night worrying about him, he could just think again!

AT THE SOUND of an automobile engine in the yard, Meg jerked upright. At some point during the interminable night, she'd dozed off in the rocking chair. It was morning; bright golden sunlight streamed through the gap in the curtains.

Rising quickly, she stepped to the window and peeked out. Jesse stood in the yard beside his truck. As she watched, he yawned and stretched his arms above his head, his movements restricted by his short denim jacket.

Where has he been all night?

Meg whirled away from the window, all her anger and hurt rushing back. The answer seemed obvious; he'd been at Joe Bob's Hell-on-the-Handbasket Guest Ranch. The real question was, had he been with anybody except the proprietor?

Walking into the bathroom, Meg leaned over the sink and threw cold water onto her face. She couldn't ask, after she'd all but ordered him to find consolation elsewhere.

But it would mean so much if he would volunteer the information. She'd believe anything he told her, no matter how unlikely. But he wouldn't tell her a thing, at least not until hell froze over—and she'd be damned if she'd ask.

So nothing had changed. There was only one way she could resurrect her fragile defenses. She must retreat once more to aloof courtesy. She must not respond to him with anger, pleasure or any other strong emotion. She must remain calm and in control.

This, too, shall pass, she counseled herself as she stepped beneath the stinging spray of the shower. *Today is Wednesday and I'm leaving Sunday, no matter what. I can do it!*

Can I do it?

It soon became apparent that Jesse had arrived at the same conclusion independently.

"GREAT DINNER, MEG. You're a heck of a good cook."

"Thank you, Jesse. It's nice of you to say so. Please, take the last piece of chicken."

"No, no, I've already had three and you just had one little old wing. You take it."

"I've had sufficient. If you don't eat it, I'll just have to throw it away."

"In that case, I'll be happy to oblige. Oh, and Meg..."

"Yes?"

"I'll wash the dishes tonight."

"That really isn't necessary."

"I insist."

"Then I accept with pleasure."

Only there was no pleasure to it, Meg thought as she went to bed hungry and miserable Wednesday night. She felt as if she were, in Thom T.'s words, "cutting off her nose to spite her face."

"WHAT IS IT Randy wants?"

Meg, sitting on the bank of Handbasket Creek with a paperback in her hand, looked up in surprise. She'd been watching squirrels scamper up and down the trunk of a nearby tree, trying to avoid thinking about her problems. As a result, she hadn't heard Jesse's approach.

Now she frowned. "What every other seven-year-old boy wants, I suppose. The newest video game, chocolate cake for dinner every day and—" She stopped short.

Jesse hunkered down beside her. "And two parents?" he supplied.

She bit her lip and stared down at the colorful cover of the book in her lap. "N-no. Many of his friends live in one-parent households."

"That doesn't make it all right, though."

Surprised by his critical tone, she gave him a quick glance. His expression remained stoic but she saw his lips tighten. "No," she agreed. "That doesn't make it all right. It just makes it understandable."

"I see." He braced his forearms on his thighs. "Then what's the third thing you think he wants?"

"I know what *I* want—not to start anything with you," she said evasively. "You'll take it as a criticism."

"I asked."

"So you did." She swallowed hard. "I think Randy would like to…have his father around once in a while, and not just for special occasions." She rushed on before he could respond. "I've explained things to him, Jesse. I really have. I haven't tried to lay everything on you."

"What 'things' have you explained?"

"Oh, that we're apart by mutual agreement. That—"

"Hold on, Meg. Mutual agreement?"

"What else?" She cocked her head to one side and frowned. "I've told him we both love him and want what's best for him, that we'll always be there for him. It's just we won't often be there *together*. I . . . I think he understands."

"How could he? *We* don't understand." Jesse heaved a great sigh and shook his head wearily. "It's starting to sound like what's best for the boy would be worst for us."

The word "reconciliation" remained unspoken; he couldn't even say the word as a remote possibility, Meg thought bitterly. But she spoke calmly. "He's just a child. He doesn't realize that two separate but happy parents is better than one miserable couple."

"Separate but happy? Riiight." Jesse's eyes narrowed to accusing slits. "Sounds like you've given this considerable thought."

Yes, oh, yes, she'd done that, both before and after arriving at this torture chamber in the Texas hills. She shrugged. "Not much else to do around here," she said flatly. She stood up and dusted off the seat of her jeans. "I think I'll fix a pitcher of lemonade. Would you like some?"

"What I'd like is some straight talk for a change." He, too, stood up. "Meg, does Randy want to go to that highfalutin school?"

In the act of turning away, she stopped. He was the boy's father and deserved an honest answer. "No," she said at last. "But I've got to try something. I do everything I can for him. I work as a volunteer instead of at a regular job so I'll always be available. I'm always there for him, but it never seems to be enough."

Her halting words came from her heart. Perhaps she should have said these things to him long ago, but she'd been afraid—still was. Afraid he'd think she wasn't a good mother, afraid she'd lose her advantage where Randy was concerned....

Jesse's expression was tense, but his voice remained gentle and nonthreatening. "Why didn't you talk to me about this a long time ago?"

"I couldn't." She began to walk slowly toward the cabin and he fell in beside her. "I kept thinking he was just going through a stage, that time was the answer." *As I foolishly thought time was the answer for us.*

How could I let my child go down the drain the same way I watched my marriage slip away?

She whirled onto the path ahead of him, desperately searching his face for any encouragement. "I'm talking to you now. Help me. Help Randy. If you don't think this school's the answer, come up with a better one."

She could see the wheels turning behind his clear eyes. He started to speak, hesitated, shook his head.

She uttered a peal of bitter laughter. "Not so easy, is it?"

"Not so hard," he retorted. "I can think of a couple of solutions, neither of which you'll like."

The cold finger of fear skipped down her spine. She shivered and turned away quickly. "Then I don't want to hear."

"Meg, you've got to hear."

"I don't see why." She opened the back door and walked into the kitchen area. "I don't want to fight with you, Jesse. I'm trying very hard to be civilized about this. I thought you were, too."

He nodded, sitting down at the table to watch her prepare the lemonade. "Meg, Randy needs to spend more time with his daddy. And I want to spend more time with him."

"You what?" She flung back her head and stared at him in confusion. "You mean—" she swallowed hard "—you want to come to Boston more often and...?"

He shook his head. "No way, José! One way is for Randy to come to me, spend time at the ranch in Showdown, go to school with real kids—"

"Go to school in Texas? Never!"

"Don't come unglued. I said that was one way."

"It's unacceptable, Jesse." She was trembling so hard she lost her hold on the lemons and they rolled across the counter and fell to the floor. "I couldn't stand it. He's all I've got and I love him more than—"

"I love him, too, and a boy needs a father, as well as a mother. Randy needs *me* and I..." Jesse's face looked vulnerable and open. "I need him. There's another way—"

"Don't say any more!" She moved, hands rising as if to fend him off although he hadn't stirred from his chair. She could just imagine what "another way" might be: divorce, a custody fight, bitterness turning to hatred—no! Desperate words poured from her heart. "You say one more thing to me on this subject and I'll walk out of here and never speak to you again as long as I live, I swear it."

"You don't mean that."

"Don't test me!"

They glared at each other for what seemed an eternity. Then Jesse rose from his chair.

"We'll talk again when you've had a chance to calm down."

"I don't intend to calm down, not about this. I don't intend to give it another thought—period."

Which naturally meant she thought of little else.

"THIS PIE IS GREAT."

"It's nothing, really. The crust came from a mix."

"Well, the filling's great, too. Pumpkin's my favorite."

"Oh? I thought apple was your favorite."

"That's my second favorite. Pumpkin's my first favorite."

"I see. Well, the filling's a mix, too."

"No kidding! Did you actually pour it into the pan and put it in the oven?"

"That, I did."

"Hell of a good job. Can I have another piece?"

SATURDAY MORNING, Jesse went for a ride and Meg was left to prowl restlessly around the cabin. *Tomorrow I'll be going home,* she reminded herself. *I mustn't weaken now.*

The strained courtesy between them had not let up. Before she drove away tomorrow, she knew she must end it by confronting an issue she'd avoided too long.

Divorce.

It was the only answer. But with that acknowledgment, she put the subject out of her mind; it was either that or go mad. She'd read every book she'd brought with her—her favorites more than once. There was no television, no telephone in the cabin. She was left to rely on her own resources and hadn't realized until now how limited they were.

Then she remembered the small trunk of mementos and the letters inside, bound by faded ribbon. The stiff paper crackled as she extracted the first sheet and smoothed it out on the table. She began to read.

Jones, Texas, August 26, 1875
My Dear Friend Diana,
I take pen in hand to inform you that our unanticipated but fortuitous meeting of the 2nd was most gratifying to your humble servant... I shall

be in San Antonio again next month on ranch
business and anticipate finding you without prior
engagements...

> Your New But Devoted Friend,
> James Taggart

San Antonio, Texas, October 2
Dear Mr. Taggart,
Almost two weeks have elapsed since that unfortunate incident with Mr. Freddy Templeton. In
that brief period, you have bombarded me with
eleven letters and five flower arrangements, not
to mention three boxes of candy which I never eat
for reasons of health. Please, Mr. Taggart, I beg
you to take pity on me, my family, the fine gen-
tlemen of the postal delivery service and the unfortunate tradesmen who have been humiliated by
my refusal to accept your insulting gratuities.
Cease and desist at once or I shall be forced to
refer this matter to my father, the judge! In your
heart you must know that the chasm between us
is far too great for earnest friendship to blossom
into any deeper emotion.

> In Distress I Remain,
> Miss Diana Lindsey

October 11
My Dearest Friend Diana,
I have closely perused your letter of October 2nd
and find myself unable to credence your pose of
indifference, in view of what transpired on the

veranda at a certain time on a certain date. Perhaps the fault is mine in not making it clear to you the honorable nature of my intentions. Do not shrink at the prospect of leaving behind the so-called comforts of civilization! There is more to happiness than the dull routine of polite society. When ranch affairs are in order I will come for you and make you my wife, for you are, and will forever remain, my only love.

Affectionately and Devotedly,
James

Where was Diana's response? Surely it must be here, yet the next letter in the stack was an inconsequential social note dated November 1889. From a Mrs. Jeb Smith, something about meeting unexpectedly at an opera in San Francisco. Meg reached for the next envelope and, beginning to read, sighed with relief.

October 25
Sir:
You must not write such things to me, or say them or even think them! I have written you two letters which I have been unable to post, fearing one to be too brutal and the other too kind to convey accurately my true feelings. Now I must cast caution to the wind and inform you that Mr. Freddy Templeton, whom you perhaps recall, has asked for my hand in holy matrimony... I have promised him an answer by Thanksgiving Day. Please have the decency in future to refrain from gratuitous references to certain innocent transgressions on my part. Nor do I grant you the right

to allude in any way to a future in which I am a participant. I beg you, Mr. Taggart, to do the right thing!

Sincerely,
Miss Lindsey

November 10

My Dearest Love Diana,

Your letter of the 25th received nearly a week ago and greeted with consternation perhaps not evident in the tardiness of this reply. After prolonged thought, I can only conclude that you are testing my sincerity. I will therefore present myself on your doorstep the day before Thanksgiving to press my suit with your father. If my sentiments in this matter seem impetuous to you in view of the fact that we have spent but scant time in each other's company, rest assured that such is not the case. There is a bond between us that death alone can sever. I sensed it the first moment my dazzled eyes beheld you.

Be forewarned, my darling girl, that you will be mine. Further know that the men of the Taggart family are faithful unto death. My love for you is immutable and everlasting. You will be my wife.

Yours forever, I remain,
James

Meg drew a ragged breath and bit down on her lower lip to control the trembling of her chin. *The men of the Taggart family are faithful unto death*—true then, perhaps, but now? She swallowed back the lump in her throat. *There is a bond between us that death alone can sever*—true of James and Diana more than a century ago; true of Jesse and Meg today?

Time to find the answers was running out.

Meg knew she and Jesse had to face the truth about their marriage today, for tomorrow they'd go their separate ways, perhaps forever. And because of that knowledge, when Jesse returned and told her he was off to Joe Bob's barbecue, Meg panicked and announced she, too, had been invited—and would join him.

THE PARTY WAS in full swing by the time Meg and Jesse arrived at the Hell-on-the-Handbasket Guest Ranch. Meg had never been there before, so she had no point of reference. But what she saw now was impressive.

Everything was as bright and spiffy as paint and planning could make it. The original house had been enlarged, presumably for guests. A long low structure nearby declared itself "Bunkhouse," but was far too fancy for that purpose and doubtless accommodated dudes.

The barbecue stood in the shade of a small grove of trees off to one side. Held waist-high by a brick support, the grill was bigger than a king-size bed. A variety of meats sizzled and hissed as Joe Bob himself applied sauce with a long-handled brush that he dipped repeatedly in a bucket simmering on the edge of the grill.

An eclectic group of individuals clustered around the chef—all ages from young to old, a variety of dress from genuine western to dude duds to California resort chic. Others lounged beneath a canopy where a western band tuned up, then began to play.

Joe Bob glanced away from his task and gave Jesse a broad grin. "Howdy, yawl." His gaze flicked to Meg and the grin slipped. Somehow her presence seemed to throw him off balance. "Howdy, Maggie," he said in a cautious voice. "Will wonders never cease."

His reaction puzzled her, but she gave him a sweet smile just the same. He seemed almost shocked to see her here with Jesse. "Your invitation was too gracious to pass up," she said dryly.

"Yeah, and I got some swampland in Florida that might interest you." He plunked the brush back into the bucket of sauce. "Hear you're leavin' us tomorrow. Shame."

Meg darted a frown at Jesse before replying. "All good things must come to an end."

"My sentiments exactly."

Jesse shifted impatiently. "You two just gettin' it out of your system or you plan to snipe at each other all day?"

Meg and Joe Bob looked at each other and announced in unison, "All day!" It was so childish that they both burst out laughing.

"I'm willin' to be civil if you are," he offered. "Hell, it's only one day!"

He wiped his hand on the apron snugged around his bulging middle before offering it to her. After the briefest of hesitations, Meg accepted his overture.

Still, she had to wonder what was going on.

But then Suzi Sherman sidled up to Jesse and rose on tiptoes to give him a friendly nip on the ear, and

Meg forgot all about Joe Bob. Jesse, to his credit, recoiled as if he'd been bitten by a snake.

Maybe too quickly? Don't be ridiculous, Meg
scolded herself. Jesse had done absolutely nothing to
encourage the woman's attentions—not that she appeared to need encouragement. She was obviously a
born flirt. Casting him a teasing glance, Suzi turned
her attentions to Joe Bob, putting her arms around his
waist as if she owned him.

Maybe she did. Meg hoped so.

A matronly woman clad in faded jeans and rundown western boots approached, an enormous metal
bucket in her arms. "Howdy, honey," she greeted
Jesse. "Now that I see her up close, your little wife
don't look a thing like Carter Dobbins's oldest gal."
The smile she turned on Meg was warm and friendly.

"Howdy, Ida Mae." Jesse took the bucket from
her; it contained beans in a sauce that smelled heav-
enly. He glanced at Meg. "This is—"

"I remember," Meg said. "Ida Mae Tuttle, from
the Lone Star Texasburger. I'm very happy to meet
you."

Ida Mae beamed. "Same here, honey." She added
to Jesse, "Tote them beans over to the picnic tables for
me, will you, honey?" Without a pause, she turned
back to Meg, as if sure Jesse would comply—which he
did. "I been wantin' to meet you ever since you and
J.J. tied the knot," she announced.

"I . . . I haven't spent much time here," Meg said
uncertainly.

Ida Mae frowned. "You know, that's right, now
you point it out. We had the idea yawl was stuck up,
but now that I think on it, that don't seem to be the

case at all. Yawl was only here for your honeymoon. Can't much be blamed for not socializin' on that occasion."

She shot a puzzled glance at Joe Bob, and all of a sudden Meg realized he'd been spreading gossip about her—apparently for years.

Ida Mae shrugged. "Well, be that as it may, Joe Bob's not payin' me to stand around and chew the fat. I gotta go make that potata salad." She grimaced. "Eat the beans. They're larrupin'."

They were that good and better. So was everything else, including the potato salad. Joe Bob presided over the buffet-style service, slicing the savory chunks of barbecued beef, separating the crusty ribs into manageable portions, cutting the sausages.

Ida Mae served the salads, the beans, the corn on the cob and the biscuits, beaming as she piled Meg's plate high. Seated between Jesse and a woman who sold real estate in San Francisco, Meg found herself slowly relaxing. Perhaps it was the feeling of inevitability that settled over her.

Her marriage would soon end, in name, as well as in fact. There seemed no point in clinging to past grievances or responding in familiar ways. None of that mattered now. She had lost him.

On the way home from the barbecue, she'd tell him that Monday she would file for divorce in Boston. He would be free, free to pursue Suzi or anyone else who caught his fancy.

A bittersweet feeling of peace enveloped her. As long as she held herself aloof, she'd be all right.

And so when Joe Bob sent some unsuspecting dude over to ask Meg how well she knew the Kennedys, she didn't bat an eye. When Suzi sidled up and announced she wanted to "borrow your handsome husband" for a dance, Meg didn't bat an eye.

When Jesse looked at her askance and asked if she was feeling all right, she didn't bat an eye.

But when he shrugged and put his arm around Suzi's waist to lead her onto the wooden dance floor, Meg turned away and walked over to the corral. Propping her foot on the bottom rail and leaning her arm against the top, she stared at the horses milling around inside.

The setting sun blinded her and she closed her eyes, her thoughts on Jesse. He, too, seemed subdued today, not even participating in Joe Bob's tomfoolery. Perhaps, as had been the case so often in the past, he was coming independently to the same conclusion she had reached.

For his pride, she hoped so. For her pride, she hoped not.

It was much later before they came together again— over the lemonade pitcher. "You're not drinking beer today?" she inquired.

He refilled her glass, then his own. "I figured I'd better keep my wits about me," he said gloomily. He drank, then licked his lips. "You seem . . . a little off your feed yourself."

She shrugged. "Not really. I'm simply a bit distracted. I have a lot on my mind. You do, too, I expect."

"You got that right." He set down his empty glass with more force than necessary. "Let me know when you're ready to leave."

"I'll do that."

She watched him walk away, weaving through the knots of people, and wished she'd told him she was ready to leave now. But she was loathe to go, for this would very likely be the last social event she ever attended with him.

Night fell. Joe Bob lit a bonfire and everyone gathered around, singing along when a guitar player struck up a tune. Staring into the flames, Meg's melancholy grew.

A log snapped and crackled, shooting a spray of sparks high into the air. The display reminded her of the fireworks on the Fourth of July. Lifting her face to follow the pinpoints of light, she looked across the circle and saw Jesse watching her with an alert questioning expression.

Her breath caught and she stared at him. In the reflection of the flames, his face looked like a sculptured work of art, all light and shadow. A yearning swept over her, almost too strong to resist—a yearning to run to him and throw her arms around him and tell him this was all a horrible mistake.

She had never intended to leave him permanently. She'd wanted to teach him a lesson, that was all. If only she had another chance.

But even as she tensed her muscles to rise, she saw Suzi ease down beside him. She said something, and he turned sharply toward her; Meg could see the seriousness of their expressions, see their lips move as they talked. She lowered her gaze quickly, eyes misty, and joined in the singing.

A few minutes later when Jesse suggested they head for home, she nodded with calm acceptance of her fate.

SILVER MOONLIGHT illuminated a night of breathless beauty. Riding beside Jesse as he drove toward the cabin, Meg sighed and leaned her elbow out the window, propping her chin on her fist. "You're awfully quiet tonight," she said into the heavy silence.

"Thinking." He said the one word abruptly, as if he resented the necessity of speaking at all.

They rode a mile more and then she said, "I had a pleasant time. Everyone was very nice to me."

"Except Joe Bob." He sounded grim.

She turned her head to look at him in dark profile. "Hey, Joe Bob is…Joe Bob. For him, that was nice."

"He's my friend." Said with stubborn determination.

"No, you're *his* friend." Under the circumstances, she might as well speak her mind; tomorrow she'd be gone. "You've given him a lot, Jesse. You've fought his battles and dragged him home when he was drunk and smoothed the feathers he's ruffled. But what's he ever done for you?"

"Any damned thing I asked!"

"That's right. But you never asked for anything, except friendship. And if it ever comes down to your welfare versus his, you'll find out whether or not Joe Bob Brooks is your buddy."

He made a left-hand turn onto the dirt road leading to the cabin. "Joe Bob's not what's been on my mind all night."

"I know." Meg bit her lower lip to still its trembling. She steeled herself. *Here it comes. This is where he says he's tired of pretending this is a marriage and he wants that divorce.*

"Think so? I doubt it. I surely do doubt it."

He slammed on the brakes so unexpectedly that she was thrown forward, catching herself with her hands on the dashboard.

He turned off the lights, killed the engine and shifted toward her on the bench seat. He drew a deep rasping breath—and said nothing.

The least she could do was help him. Feeling sorry for both of them, she patted his hand where it rested on the seat between them. "Go ahead," she invited gently. "Say what you have to say. I promise I won't scream or yell or throw things."

"You do?" His puzzled voice came out of the darkness.

"I do. We've already hurt each other so much, I'd really like to make this as painless as possible." *Hang on,* she cautioned herself. *You're doing fine. Don't cave in now.* "So just say it. I'm ready."

She braced herself, unconsciously tightening her hand over his. Out of the velvety night she heard his voice as if from far away.

"You're right. I'm about to do something I swore I'd never do, so I might as well bite the bullet." He drew another ragged breath.

Meg sat very still. It was torture, having it dragged out this way. "Just say what you have to say," she blurted. "If you want a divorce, you'll have to ask for it." She took a deep breath and tried to see him in the darkness. "That's it, isn't it? You want to end this marriage."

"Hell no!" he shot back. "I'm trying to get up the nerve to..." He groaned. "Meggie, I'm trying to get up the nerve to ask you to give our marriage another try."

CHAPTER EIGHT

MEG BEGAN TO TREMBLE. Surely she'd heard wrong. He couldn't have said...

Jesse pressed her shoulder, his fingers digging into her tense muscles with fierce insistence. "I never got over you, Meggie," he said as if making some shameful confession. "I wanted to—Lord knows I wanted to. I tried."

"'The men of the Taggart family are faithful unto death'—that's what your great-great-grandfather James wrote to your great-great-grandmother Diana." Could that calm voice be hers?

Jesse groaned. "He was right. I knew the moment I saw you that you're the only woman for me."

He slid his hands up the slope of her shoulder until he could curve his fingers around the back of her neck. With his thumb he rubbed the pulse throbbing at the base of her throat.

Meg shivered. Everything in her screamed a warning; *if you move, this moment will vanish in a puff of smoke and you'll find yourself on an airplane headed for Boston.* "You're doing this for Randy," she suggested, afraid to think otherwise.

"Hell, no!" He stroked the side of her face, the line of her jaw, the curve behind her ear. "I'm doing it—trying to do it—for us. Because I don't think you're over me, either. I think you've missed me just as much as I missed you, but you're too stubborn to admit it.''

With pressure on the back of his neck, he drew her stiff figure toward him. She went with a sigh.

''Who's stubborn?'' she whispered. Swamped by the tide of love she'd fought so long, she cupped his face between her hands. In the dim interior of the pickup, she could barely make out his features.

She didn't need to see him with her eyes; she held his image fast in her heart. The lean handsome face and clear gray eyes, the high cheekbones and wide sensuous mouth—individual features that added up to the face of her husband, the man she loved.

He smoothed the short curls away from her face. ''When it comes to stubborn, we're a match if there ever was one. Way I figure it, somebody's got to make the first move or we'll be old and gray before we admit we were meant to be together.''

He turned his head and pressed his lips against her tender palm, which was still cupping his face. ''I want you to be my wife again,'' he said into the breathless silence.

Meg's heart skipped a beat and then took off like a rocket. ''I've always been your wife,'' she insisted.

He shook his head impatiently. ''I mean in every sense of the word, and you damn well know it. I want you back in my house and my bed. When we have a problem, I don't want you two or three thousand miles away—and I don't ever want you walkin' out on me again! I want you to be there for me and I want to be there for you. Always.''

''Y-you want a lot.'' Her words were sheer bravado.

''I'm willing to give a lot to get it.''

Her mind whirled. "Anything else?"

"Hell, yes! I want an answer to my proposal."

"Okay."

They sat there rigidly in the dark and time stretched out between them. She could feel his tension increase in the pressure of his palms against the backs of her hands, and then he shifted restlessly on his seat.

At last he said, "Okay what? This is no joke—I need an answer, Meggie. You comin' home where you belong?"

"Oh, Jesse!" Laughter bubbled in her throat and she flung herself against his chest. "That *was* my answer—okay! Okay means yes. I'm in such a state of shock maybe I'm not making sense."

He let out a whoop of victory and dragged her onto his lap. Twisting his fingers through her short curls, he rained kisses on her cheek and throat. "You think *you're* in shock! I was afraid you'd slap my face and tell me to get outta town."

"And I thought..." She felt his arms tighten, his breath fan the strands of hair covering her ear. "I thought you'd finally had enough and were about to ask for a divorce."

"Taggarts don't divorce."

His mouth found hers at last, at long last. It was the kiss she'd been waiting for. The magic had never failed her and it didn't fail her now. Only Jesse could make her weak and willing with a single kiss. Thus had it ever been; thus would it ever be, she supposed.

His hand touched the bare skin of her midriff beneath the hem of her blouse. She jumped as if burned and her pulse rate accelerated.

"J-Jesse?"

His reply was muffled because his lips were pressed against her throat. "Ummm?"

It took all her strength to speak and, even then, she couldn't keep her voice firm. "Why are we sitting in a pickup truck in the middle of a dirt road in the middle of the night in the middle of nowhere when we could be home... together?"

"You mean in bed, making love." His torso shuddered with suppressed laughter. "Ever the little pragmatist, aren't you? What if I told you I didn't want to wait until we get back to the cabin to make love to you?" He punctuated his question by trailing his hands in lazy strokes across her back and sides.

She shivered. "I'd say... neither do I, but I don't think we're acrobatic enough to pull it off in the cab of a truck."

"Then we'll have to think of something else." His delight warmed her. He tightened his grip on her waist. "Meggie, I love you," he said, sounding suddenly serious. "I was a damned fool to let you get away from me, and I won't make that mistake again. You understand that, don't you?"

"If I say yes does that mean I've just agreed to make love in a pickup truck?"

"Nope. It means you agree we—" his teasing laughter washed over her "—deserve each other."

"Oh, yes. Yes." Her gasp of acquiescence included agreement both with his words and with the feelings he aroused in her with his hands.

Still, she was completely unprepared when he threw open the truck door. Blinking in the harsh glare of the dome light, she saw his eyes glitter with barely suppressed excitement. His mouth curved in a smile and he held out his hand.

She hesitated. Despite all the serious intent below the bantering surface, she hadn't thought for a minute that they would make love anywhere except in a proper bed.

"Come with me," he said in a voice as warm and sweet as melted caramel.

She gazed up at him for a long moment, then put her hand in his with utter trust. He lifted her out of the vehicle. Reaching back inside, he gave a tug and dragged out a plaid blanket.

She leaned weakly against the open door. "What are we doing? We must be crazy!" She glanced around as if expecting an avalanche of disapproval.

"Nobody here but you, me, and maybe a few cows or jackrabbits," he assured her. "Where's your spirit of adventure? I'll bet you've never made love anyplace in your life except in a bed."

Even in the darkness, she felt her face flush—not because of what he said but because of what he darned well should know. She clenched a fist and smacked him on the shoulder. "You know *exactly* where I've made love because you've been there every single time!"

"Oh, yeah, that's right," he teased. Drawing her aside, he slammed the pickup door.

She turned to him and slid her arms around his waist. "I guess you know I...love you," she said shyly, her words muffled.

He stood very still. "Yes, I know. But I wasn't sure you did."

She nodded. "I do—I've always known. I love you, Jesse. *I love you!*" She rose on tiptoe and kissed his throat, feeling his pulse hammer beneath her lips.

"Then come with me now," he said in a voice heavy with promise. "Trust me, and come with me now."

He led her through the grasses, beneath the trees, to the banks of Handbasket Creek. Where he had shown her the deer on Independence Day, he spread the blanket.

Perhaps it was the totality of commitment or the rebirth of hopes and dreams all but dead. Whatever it was, she longed to surrender to him more completely and freely than she had ever done before. And somehow she sensed an answering depth of feeling in him.

As he knelt beside her, she saw a metallic flash in the moonlight and caught his hand between hers. "W-wait a minute," she gasped. "There's something I have to know."

"Later," he suggested in a husky voice.

"Now, Jesse. Please." She touched the third finger of his left hand. "Tell me—why are you wearing your wedding ring? Did you put it on because Thom T. forced you to come here?"

He groaned but made no attempt to avoid an answer, as she might have expected. "I'd like to say I kept it on because I was sure we'd get back together someday."

She licked her lips. "But that wouldn't be true, would it?"

He shook his head. "No, that wouldn't be true. After the first couple of years, I figured a snowball'd have a better chance in hell than our marriage had of surviving."

"So you took off your ring." They weren't touching at all now. How she longed to be back in his arms!

He shook his head. "I never took off my ring. Did you?"

"Of course not."

"I suppose you wore your ring for Randy's sake." He sounded sad.

That reason had never occurred to her, but now that he suggested it, it made perfect sense. Only that wasn't the case at all. "I—"

"That's okay," he interrupted quickly. "You asked first and you deserve an answer." He hesitated, then spoke in a rush, as if embarrassed by what he was about to say.

"At first I thought you'd be back. Damn, I was sure of it. Then when I realized you meant business, I considered taking off my ring but...hell, I decided it was too good a shield against predatory females."

She swallowed hard. "And it worked?"

"Sometimes. At first, anyway. Lately it seems to be losing its power."

"Oh." She could barely force out the one word.

There was a long pause and then, "I'm lying," he whispered. "I kept the damned ring on because I never lost hope that someday we'd be together again—like this."

THEY LAY TOGETHER side by side on the blanket, hands clasped, staring up between the leafy boughs of trees. Labored breathing had slowly returned to normal, and once more Meg heard the murmur of Handbasket Creek. By turning her head, she could catch the gleam of moonlight on lazily moving water.

Jesse rolled onto his side. "You're beautiful," he said in a fiercely possessive voice. "It always takes me by surprise, how beautiful you are. You dress so prim and proper and you never flirt or lead men on, but underneath you've got enough fire to burn Chicago down all over again—hell, Dallas even!''

Meg smiled lazily. "I appreciate your testimonial but I'm no Suzi Sherman," she said.

"Suzi who?" He leaned over, blotting out the sky and everything else in the universe besides the two of them.

"I'LL FLY BACK to Boston with you tomorrow. We'll tell Randy together.''

"Oh, Jesse, he'll be so happy!" Meg moved closer, snuggling against him.

He tightened his arms around her as if he would never let her go. "He's not the only one. I suspect even those two old reprobate grandpas of ours will heave a sigh of relief over this.''

"Really?" She was doubtful and it showed. "I never thought Thom T. liked me.''

"He never knew you, hon. But he loves our son, and that means he'll lean over backward to accommodate you. Once you get to know each other, he'll be crazy about you. Just don't try to be *too* nice or he'll mistake it for weakness, if you get my drift.''

She did. She wished he'd given her this advice eight years ago.

His voice turned dubious. "*Your* grandpa, now— that's a different kettle of fish.''

"He's a pussycat!''

"He controls fortunes, political and financial, and you call him a pussycat?''

"No, sweetheart," she teased, "I call him Grandpa and so does Randy. You may call him 'sir.'" She giggled and dropped a quick kiss on his chin. "Seriously—''

"You *were* serious—don't try to kid me."

"Seriously, he just wants Randy and me to be happy. If that makes you happy in the process, he can probably learn to live with it."

"Hell of a guy."

"Sarcasm doesn't become you—ah! But that does..."

THEY PULLED UP to the cabin as the sun rose, signaling much more than simply the start of a new day in Meg's entranced state of mind. She felt as if she were embarking on a new life of endless promise.

Jesse turned off the engine and grinned at her. He didn't look the least bit tired, despite his lack of sleep. Meg smiled; she hadn't had any more sleep than he'd had and she felt wonderful!

He reached out to touch one tangled curl, his long-lashed eyes half closing. "You look sexy as hell," he murmured, "all tousled and sleepy-eyed and gorgeous. Makes me want to—"

"—close up the cabin so we can get this show on the road." She held him off with one hand. "If we hurry, we can leave today." Eager to get started, she reached for the passenger door.

"Hold it!"

As she straightened in surprise he jumped out of the truck, sprinted around the front and yanked open her door. He held out his arms.

She frowned suspiciously. "What are you up to?"

"I just want to carry you over the threshold so we can get our second marriage off on the right foot, so to speak."

"So to speak."

She slid close enough to allow him to scoop her into his arms. He carried her up the steps and across the porch and pushed open the unlocked door.

And then he carried her inside and down the hall and into the bedroom. Before she could protest, she had no breath left to protest *with*—not to mention anything to protest about.

IT WAS ALMOST TEN that morning before they got around to eating. Both were ravenous, so Meg fried potatoes and sausage, scrambled eggs and baked biscuits, brewed coffee and stirred up a can of frozen orange juice. They consumed the meal with gusto.

Meg watched him butter another biscuit. "So," she said, determined to get down to business. "What do we have to do to get this place ready to close it up?"

Jesse's lips gleamed with melted butter and his tongue flicked out to lick it away. "First thing I've got to do is gather the stock," he said. "Shouldn't take too long unless that far fence in the east pasture's down again. I've had a devil of a time keeping that sorrel in. I'll either have to go by Joe Bob's place now or we can stop on our way out, but I've got to tell him I won't be around to give him a hand with the big chuck-wagon supper he's plannin' for next weekend."

"Poor Joe Bob. What a shame." She gave Jesse an artless smile, which didn't appear to fool him in the slightest. "What do I need to do in here?"

He gestured vaguely. "The usual—pack, strip the beds. Thom T.'ll have someone standing by to do the real cleaning."

"Okay." She began to stack the dirty dishes. "I think I'll run a couple of loads of laundry. I hate to mix clean things with dirty when I pack. Give me your stuff, too." She looked up sharply, frowning. "What've you been doing for clean clothes? I haven't been doing your laundry, and I know *you* haven't used the washing machine."

He looked uncomfortable. "I, uh, took it to a friend."

"A friend!" Visions of blond temptresses flashed through Meg's head and she clenched her lips together. "Anyone I know?"

The easy good humor left his face. "You're pushing."

She lifted her chin a notch. "You call that pushing? If I wanted to push, I'd ask you where you went the other night, after we . . . had our little differences. You didn't get home until dawn." She raised one brow. "Now that I think about it, much the same as today." *But the reason damned well better not be the same,* she thought fiercely.

"And if I wanted to push back, I'd—" He stopped short, his eyes flashing. With an obvious effort, he controlled himself. "Now isn't the time to get into this," he said with finality. "But it is something we'll have to deal with."

"You mean . . . ?" She stopped, confused and sorry she'd started anything. Did he mean he *had* done something that night that had to be dealt with? Or did he mean they had to deal with their unfortunate tendency to leap to conclusions and stubbornly refuse to clear up misunderstandings?

If they were misunderstandings. She shivered. She hadn't really believed he'd done anything wrong that night, but now she wasn't so sure. Wherever the truth lay, she couldn't confront it now. She wanted to bask a little longer in her newfound happiness.

For now, she wanted to believe in happy endings—needed to believe. "Yes," she agreed quickly, "this isn't the time."

He looked surprised, but his smile made everything all right. He came around the table and took her in his arms. "I hate to leave you," he murmured, nuzzling her hair. "You sure we don't have time...?"

She laughed despite the tightness in her throat. "I love you, Jesse James Taggart. You're incorrigible, but I love you."

"Is that a yes?"

"That's not even a maybe!" She gave him a squeeze and pulled away. "There'll be lots of time for that later. Right now there's a little boy waiting for us in Boston. I, for one, can't tell him the good news soon enough."

Jesse cocked his head to one side and his eyes gleamed. He pulled her close, his hand pressing low against her spine. "As my sainted grandpa used to say, 'Never put off till tomorrow what—'"

"Jesse!"

"I'm going, I'm going!"

And after a quick but fiery kiss, he did.

DESPITE HER DESIRE to work efficiently, Meg drifted through her chores. Pulling the sheets from the double bed she and Jesse had shared, she found herself standing there with the fabric clutched against her breast, a silly smile on her face. Laughing, she threw the sheet aside and reached for the next one.

She carried the laundry through the dining area and into the alcove where the washer and dryer were. Tossing in the sheets, she headed for the small bedroom where Jesse had slept *before*.

Dragging off his sheets, she turned toward the door. A wad of pants and shirts near the foot of the bed caught her eye and she grimaced. Was it only Jesse, or did all men think of the floor as a great natural clothes hamper? She leaned down, scooped up the pile and carried it with her to the washing machine.

Of course, they had many things more important than sloppiness still to discuss. She was confident they could reach agreement in the spirit of compromise. She began to sort, emptying out pockets as she went: whites, colors, permanent press, denim.

When you loved and trusted someone, all things were possible, she thought complacently. She believed that with all her heart and soul—now.

Love and trust. Yes! She laughed out loud, crushing Jesse's denim jacket in a hug meant for him. When they leveled with each other—when he accepted how important honest communication was to her—he'd change his ways, she was sure of it. And if there was some little insignificant thing she did or didn't do that he'd like her to change...

She reached into a pocket of the jacket and pulled out...something, she wasn't sure what. Something black and lacy. She stared at the bit of fabric, at first without comprehension and then with growing horror. Her hand opened as if of its own volition and the *thing* fell to the floor.

Dropping to her knees she had to force herself to touch the crushed bit of fabric, to pick it up, to shake it out...

...to identify it as a black lace T-shirt, last seen—by Meg, at any rate—covering the buxom and unfettered curves of Miss Suzi Sherman. But...but...! She searched for an explanation.

The blond bombshell had been wearing the offending article of clothing that fateful day in the Hell's Bells Low Life Saloon.

But Suzi had left the saloon with Joe Bob, while Meg and Jesse had left together! They'd had a lovely dinner, after which they'd come back to this very cabin and... had one hell of a row.

Too clearly Meg remembered her own voice shouting, "You'll have to find yourself another playmate... You already know where to look!"

And his answer: "You got *that* right!"

He'd driven away in his pickup, returning the following day with the dawn. Could there be any doubt now where he'd gone?

Could there be any doubt who'd been doing his laundry?

Could there be any doubt that nothing at all had changed since that horrible, horrible night five years ago?

Crouching on the floor before the washing machine, déjà vu of the worst sort rushed over Meg....

SHE'D LOOKED AT HIM in horror. "Jesse! There's lipstick on your collar!"

"So send it to the laundry. They can get anything out these days."

"I don't care about your stupid shirt! I want to know how the lipstick got there!"

She'd had every right to ask. But Jesse's mouth thinned in that familiar stubborn way, and his eyes narrowed into slits in his tired dusty face.

"I need a shower, Meg," he said with exaggerated patience. "I've just been thrown on my butt in the dirt, kicked by a horse and stomped by a bull. I sure as hell don't need to come home to a wife who—"

"What? Who thinks you should have the common decency to explain—"

"I never explain. It's a sign of weakness."

"Dear Lord, he's quoting John Wayne! Jesse! Don't walk away when I'm talking to you! Jesse—"

"I said I need a shower."

"And I said I want to know how this lipstick smudge..."

She followed him into the bathroom, railing at him. Stoically he stripped off his rodeo clothes—work clothes to him—and turned on the shower. Even in her current state of advanced fury, she had to admire the lean strength of his muscular body.

"Jesse! I demand an answer!"

"You know I can't hear you when I'm in the shower."

"You can if I'm in the shower with you!"

Steaming, shaking with anger, she flung open the shower door and plunged inside. The soles of her shoes skidded on the wet floor and she would have fallen had he not grabbed her. His eyes glittered inches from hers, water streaming over both their heads. Her linen trousers would be ruined, her silk blouse destroyed, but she didn't care.

She wanted an explanation so badly that for a moment she contemplated begging him for one. If he crushed her in his arms and told her the lipstick meant nothing, she'd believe him. She'd even try to overlook the blond hairs on his jacket a couple of weeks ago, the telephone numbers she occasionally found in his pockets, the "if a woman answers, hang up" telephone calls.

But instead she braced her palms against the slick muscles of his chest and shoved. "You owe me an explanation!"

"I owe you love. You have it. I owe you respect. You have it. I owe you faithfulness and you damned well have that, too!" He was shouting by the time he finished, his fingers biting into her arms through the limpid silk.

He gave her a none-too-gentle shake. "Well? Say something!"

She glared at him, trying to keep her attention on his face and the business at hand, not on the wetly gleaming length of him. "I'll say something!" she cried. "How did that lipstick get on the collar of your shirt? Until you answer me, we have nothing to talk about."

She took a step back—that is, her feet did, water squishing between her toes inside her shoes. But her body didn't, because he held her in such a rigid grasp.

He gave her the long slow smile that always turned her insides to mush. "Okay," he agreed. "I didn't want to talk, anyway. We'll communicate on a... higher level."

He crushed her against him, his mouth claiming hers in a sizzling kiss. She couldn't let him get away with this, she warned herself as her arms stole around his neck and her eyes closed. She wanted to resist when he smoothed the long wet hair away from her face and pressed burning kisses on wet skin.

By the time he carried her into the bedroom, the word "resist" no longer seemed to be in her vocabulary, neither mental nor verbal. But later it returned to haunt her—later, when the police called to report they'd picked up a drunken Joe Bob, when Jesse dutifully rose from bed and went to bail out his friend, when she was left alone with her toddler sleeping in the next room.

And her husband's shirt collar still smeared with lipstick...and the knowledge that he only had to touch her to get anything he wanted from her, *without* an explanation.

Until that very moment.

She'd been on her way to Boston by the time he got Joe Bob out of jail and sobered up. *If you can't fight him and you won't join him, better to avoid him entirely,* was her way of justifying what was essentially an irrational act.

Irrational, and also desperate.

CHAPTER NINE

EYES CLOUDED WITH PAIN, Meg knelt before the washing machine and looked at the bit of lace, revulsion making her stomach muscles clench. She remembered Jesse's scornful voice. "A genuine dude will believe anything."

Yes, Meg thought, *that's me, all right—a dude! If I wasn't, I wouldn't have been stupid enough to believe he loves me.*

For five interminable years, she had more or less avoided him and her feelings for him. Then through the meddling interference of two well-meaning old men, she'd been forced to confront the unalterable fact that she loved Jesse James Taggart and always would. She'd thought this time things would be different.

But if he didn't love her, why would he want to revive their marriage?

The answer was obvious: for his son's sake.

They'd both come to this godforsaken place for Randy. All the blackmail in the world wouldn't have worked without that basic underlying motive. For Randy's sake, Jesse was willing to take the boy's mother back into his life.

But the terms, as always, were his.

Could she live with that? Even loving him as she did, even realizing there would never be another man for her, could she live with that?

No!

Blinded by tears, she threw down the reprehensible bit of lace, jumped up and grabbed her purse. She didn't change her clothes, didn't pack a bag.

But she did hesitate with her hand on the door of her rental car.

With slow agonized steps she returned to the cabin. Standing over the damning piece of evidence, she twisted savagely at her golden wedding band. The ring hadn't been off her finger since the day Jesse had put it there. It didn't want to come off now.

Panic overwhelmed her—she ran to the sink and squirted dishwashing liquid on her left hand. Tugging, twisting, she pulled at the reluctant ring, which suddenly seemed to burn her flesh. The golden circle popped off and sailed through the air, landing without a sound on the pile of black lace.

For a moment she stared at it, through a haze of tears she could no longer hold back.

Then she turned and walked out of the cabin, slamming the door forever on that part of her life.

JESSE RODE the bay gelding up to the main house of Joe Bob's dude ranch and stepped out of the saddle. In keeping with the Wild West theme of the place, a hitching rail stood beside the walkway leading to the boss man's office. Jesse tossed the reins over the rail as Joe Bob stuck his head through the open door.

"Just in time to tie to the feed bag, cowboy."

"Much obliged but I already ate. I'll have a cup of coffee, if it's not too much trouble."

Jesse followed his host through the door, taking off his hat as he stepped inside. Without waiting for further invitation, he helped himself from the coffee urn near the door. Joe Bob returned to his messy desk and the tray of food there.

Jesse took a sip of coffee and looked around his friend's messy domain with wry amusement. Poor ol' Joe Bob really needed a keeper; shame Wanda hadn't been willing to stick it out. She'd been the best thing that ever happened to the big guy, whether he knew it or not.

Sometimes it seemed as if Joe Bob was hell-bent on his own destruction. *But he's a man grown and it's no skin off my back,* Jesse reminded himself. He flat out didn't like sticking his nose into other people's business—or having them stick their noses into his.

"What you starin' at?" Joe Bob groused. He stopped shoveling stew into his mouth to glare. "You never seen a man eat before?"

"I've seen horses eat. Same thing." Jesse moved a pile of papers to make room and took a seat on the leather couch.

"You ride all the way over here to throw rocks at poor ol' Joe Bob?"

"Nope. I rode over to tell poor ol' Joe Bob that I'm pullin' out later today. I won't be around to help you herd dudes like I promised."

Joe Bob threw down his spoon. "Well, if that don't take the cake! You're a helluva friend, you know that?"

"Yep. I know that," Jesse agreed, unruffled.

"Where you goin' to in such a all-fired hurry?" Joe Bob's eyes narrowed and then he started to smile. "I bet I know. You finally got fed up with that starchy

little Miss Priss you married. Man, I knew this big
second honeymoon was—''

"Hold it!'' The words ripped out like bullets.

Joe Bob reared back in surprise. Jesse stared at his
longtime friend, an unpleasant possibility raising its
ugly head. Joe Bob had never been Mr. Cool where
women were concerned, but this time he'd jumped to
conclusions even more hastily than usual.

What if Meg was right about him? What if he didn't
like her, had never liked her and went out of his way
to ambush and undercut her and make her life miserable? That possibility made Jesse very uncomfortable, indeed.

"Joe Bob,'' he said, "you've just shoved your foot
into your mouth up to your knee, and I have to wonder why. What exactly is it you got against Meg, anyway?''

"Why, same thing you do, I reckon,'' the big man
blustered. "Hell, I'm on your side. I'd give you the
shirt off my back, buddy. You know that. I'd give you
my right arm! You want my best horse or my best gal?
Hell, I'll call ol' Suzi in here—''

"That's enough!'' Jesse felt his scalp prickle with
distaste. He didn't like what he was hearing or thinking. "There's only one thing you can do for me.''

"Name it.'' Joe Bob threw out his arms expan-
sively.

"Apologize to my wife. You damn well owe it to
her.''

"The hell you say!'' Joe Bob hefted his bulk forward in the chair, his blue eyes wide and shocked-
looking. "You just said yawl's pullin' out on her, so
why should I—''

"I didn't say I was leaving her, I said I was leaving *here*—with her. We're going back to Boston to pick up our boy and then we'll be a family again." It felt good to say it and Jesse's anger began to fade. Joe Bob was Joe Bob. Meg was mistaken; he didn't mean any harm.

"Man, I don't owe that woman anything, least of all an apology!" Joe Bob looked and sounded desperate.

"Up to you. I don't think your chances of getting in her good graces are any too likely without one. And I'm duty bound to back her. Hell, Joe Bob, just explain that it's all been in fun and promise to lighten up on her in the future. No big thing."

"I never explain! It's a sign of weakness!"

Jesse plunked down his coffee cup on the end table and stood up. "That is just about the dumbest damn thing I ever—" He stopped short. He'd said the same thing to Meg and then wondered why she went crazy. He clapped his hat back on his head with unnecessary force. "Up to you," he said again, and turned toward the door.

"Be fair, J.J." Joe Bob followed Jesse through the door. "The woman ain't worthy of you, is the thing. I got nothin' against her personally except that. Hell, what kinda woman walks out on her man for five years like she done? You shoulda married one of our fine Texas gals...."

"Like Wanda?" Jesse spoke in a deadly soft voice.

Joe Bob's heavy face flushed. "You're hittin' low, there, buddy. Wanda didn't leave me, I—I threw her out!"

It was such a patently pitiful lie that for a moment Jesse just stood there feeling sorry for the teller. Then he shrugged. "Joe Bob," he said slowly, "you've been my friend for as long as I can remember. I never thought I'd have to say this to you."

"Aw, J.J., you ain't gonna let some woman come between old pals."

"Not some woman—my wife. I've made excuses for you for years. Hell, I believed the excuses myself. But no more. It's still your choice, but I'm tellin' you straight out—this is the end of the trail unless you apologize to Meg. And if you do it, you damned well better mean it."

Jesse untied his horse and swung onto the saddle, a movement nearly as natural to him as breathing. He turned his mount just as Suzi came out of the building. She waved at him and walked over to Joe Bob. She put her arms around his waist and stretched to kiss him on the cheek.

Joe Bob just stood there like a stick of wood, ignoring her. Jesse thought the man looked a little sick.

And then he wasn't thinking about that anymore. The woman he loved was waiting.

The woman he loved and trusted; the woman who loved and trusted him.

MEG DROVE toward San Antonio, hardly seeing the brilliant summer day through which she sped in the rental car. Had he returned to the cabin yet? she wondered. Did he realize she was gone?

If he did, did he care?

Tears blurred her eyes and she tried to blink them away. What did it matter? He wouldn't come after her; she knew that to her grief. He didn't explain, he didn't apologize, and he wouldn't come after her. There was no point in hoping that he would.

And she *was* hoping—stop it! she berated herself. How could she let this happen to her again? It almost killed her the last time. Didn't she ever learn? The man wasn't about to change and she might as well face that immutable fact.

JESSE SET THE BAY into a ground-eating lope and tried to pay attention to the job at hand, but there was no way he could concentrate on anything beyond his own elation. Damn, he didn't want to waste time chasing stock. He'd told Thom T. all they needed were a couple of good riding horses, but the old codger had brought up eight "just in case."

In case of what? Jesse wondered as he turned his horse along the banks of Handbasket Creek. In case he wanted to give riding lessons?

Whatever the reason, now Jesse was obliged to gather the small herd and pin them in the corral so Thom T.'s men could pick them up and truck them back to the home-place. Too bad they couldn't just be left here, the beginnings of a herd. That's what he'd really like to do, Jesse thought; stock this land with a few good animals, raise and train quarter horses.

With Meg and Randy at his side, it'd be a kind of heaven. He'd give up rodeo in a minute if he thought— He caught a flash of red-brown and turned his mount into a gully.

Within minutes, he'd lost track of his quarry. He reined in, standing tall in the stirrups to look around. Although this was the kind of work he loved, today his mind and his heart were elsewhere.

But not in Boston, where they'd been for so long. In the Wonderful World of Stubborn, Meg took a back seat to no one. Still, he was totally committed to her, had been even during those years when she sat in itty-bitty ol' Massachusetts, defying logic and good sense.

When she'd left him, his first inclination had been to go after her and drag her home. His second inclination, the one he followed, had been to give her time to realize how wrong she was.

He'd lost faith in that strategy years ago, so no one was more surprised than he that it had worked in the long run. Their reconciliation last night was proof positive to him that she'd realized the error of her ways.

He was right and she was wrong.

The sorrel horse appeared across the creek and Jesse gave a shout of satisfaction. He dug his heels into the sides of his mount. The pony jumped forward as the small herd burst from the trees.

Hope she's ready to go when I get back, he thought as he rode after the horses. *Wait until Randy hears!*

TRAFFIC PICKED UP as Meg neared the city. She slowed, painfully aware that she had nearly reached the point of no return. Once she stepped onto that airplane, her marriage would be finished. Contacting an attorney tomorrow in Boston would be just a formality.

San Antonio International Airport was on the north side of the city. Too soon she was guiding the car into the parking lot of the auto-rental firm.

Without baggage to worry about, she sped through the preliminaries. She felt a little awkward about traveling in jeans and T-shirt and leather sneakers— her grandfather would not be pleased when she showed up at Logan International looking like this. But as she stood in line at the ticket counter, she realized there was really nothing to feel awkward about. No one paid her the slightest attention.

She was very definitely alone.

And would be now, for the rest of her life. Boarding pass in hand, she cast about for an out-of-the-way place to wait the couple of hours before she could board the plane. She found it, a bank of inconveniently placed seats away from the mainstream, completely ignored by other travelers.

Briefly she considered buying a book or paper at the newsstand but decided it would be pointless. Who was she trying to kid? There was no way she could concentrate on anything beyond her own misery.

JESSE TURNED his small herd toward home. He was slowing himself down by trying to go too fast, he realized. The animals sensed his excitement and acted up. He had to get hold of himself.

But it was hard. Pausing to let the horses drink in Handbasket Creek, he shifted restlessly in his saddle.

Yep, he thought. *That's what I'm gonna do—get myself out of rodeo before they have to carry me out in pieces. Hell, I don't want or need the Rocking T. Everything I could ever want will be right here.*

I'll call it the Triple T for the three Taggarts—Meg, Randy and me.

Would she go for it?

Crowding the horses back onto the trail, he smiled. She might, but if she didn't, they could find some other compromise.

As long as they were together, all things were possible. She'd never run out on him again.

Never.

HAD HE RETURNED to the cabin yet? Did he know she was gone?

At this very moment, he could be banging through the rooms calling her name. She could imagine the rising note of panic in his voice—had to imagine it, because she'd never heard it. She'd never known Jesse to panic, not about anything. But if he loved her, wouldn't he feel at least a twinge of panic at losing her again?

Perversely, she hoped so, because this time it was forever. He must know it, too.

Oh, but he'd react as he had before! Of course he would, even though all he had to do—all she asked of him—was to explain. Okay, there were ways he might innocently get lipstick on his collar. But there was only one explanation for the black lace T-shirt in his pocket.

Wasn't there? If there was another explanation, it was horribly unfair of him not to make it. He'd said it himself: "If you'd found a lady's unmentionables in my pocket, that would have been another story entirely."

She had, and it was.

But then a new and unwelcome possibility presented itself: if he was making the same mistake, was she not, also, by running away again?

She pressed her knuckles to her teeth, so tense she could barely sit still. Questions buffeted her, questions of her own asking. *Am I being fair? Am I simply reacting out of habit?*

And the really big one—*Do I really believe him capable of cheating on me?*

JESSE HERDED the horses into the corral and, without dismounting, leaned down to slam the gate closed. Damned broomtails stirred up enough dust for thirty horses, he thought as he stepped down off the bay. Tossing the reins over a corral post, he turned toward the cabin—and stopped short.

Something was wrong.

It took him a moment to realize Meg's rental car was gone. Frowning, he started forward with long impatient strides, all the while telling himself there was nothing to worry about. She'd run into town for one reason or another, that was all. He'd find a note inside, he was sure of it. He'd laugh at this sick feeling of panic....

He threw open the unlocked door with unnecessary violence and called her name, just in case she'd loaned the car to someone else and was still here. Only silence greeted him.

A quick glance toward the living room showed it to be empty. He moved quickly down the hall, looking into each bedroom and finding no clues. Returning to the kitchen, he tossed his hat on the counter and scratched his head. Now what in the hell...?

His restlessly roving glance lit on a pile of dark fabric on the floor before the open folding doors to the laundry alcove. He frowned and took a cautious step forward.

He might not have looked farther had not a golden gleam caught his eye. His heart leapt erratically and he bent, reaching out with suddenly cold fingers.

Meg's wedding ring. His dry throat closed on him.

He grabbed the bit of black and shook it out. At first he couldn't even figure out what it was—some kind of top or undershirt, no bigger than a child would wear. Then he realized the damned thing stretched and he flashed on Suzi. He'd seen her wedged into something like this in the recent past.

How'd it get here? He knelt and touched the other garment lying on the floor, trying to reason this out.

His denim jacket, the one he'd worn several times since he got here. What in the hell was going on?

Automatically he reached into a jacket pocket. When he pulled out a lipstick case, he suddenly knew. He'd been set up, and only one person could have done it.

But the worst part was Meg was gone. That meant she still believed him capable of playing around.

What did that make him in Meg's eyes? What did that make Meg in his?

YET ANOTHER fifteen-minute delay in boarding— great.

Meg sank back down in her seat near the loading gate and stared at the ticket clutched in her hand. She'd been holding it so long and tightly that it was limp and pathetic.

As was she.

She'd lost her privacy. Travelers milled around her, travelers of all sizes and ages and nationalities. Couples, families . . . She looked away quickly.

Her mind kept going around in circles. Always it came back to the same point: this was her last chance with Jesse.

Why was she leaving him again when she loved him?

If he wouldn't change, could she?

"Attention, all passengers for Alar Airlines flight 333 nonstop to Boston—"

She bolted to her feet. Now was the time to decide.

CHAPTER TEN

"EXCUSE ME—please, can I get past?"

Meg plunged through the crowd, fighting the ebb and flow of travelers milling impatiently around the loading gate. Most seemed angered by the latest delay in the scheduled departure time.

She drew a few inquisitive glances as she ran down the long sloping walkway leaving the concourse. For once, curious glances didn't concern her.

Of course, a long line stood between her and the ticket counter. She hesitated, undecided; all she wanted to do now was go back to fight for her marriage. Unfortunately, her thrifty New England heritage demanded she obtain a refund on her ticket.

It'll just take a few minutes, she soothed herself. Stepping into the line, she pursed her lips impatiently and tried not to fidget.

The woman ahead of her looked around with a sympathetic smile on her pleasantly chubby face. "My sentiments exactly," she said. The line inched forward and the woman nudged her suitcase along with one foot. "Goin' far, honey?"

"Not anymore." A feeling of relief washed over her. She waved her dog-eared ticket, then stuffed it into her hip pocket and wiped damp palms on her thighs. "I'm cashing in a ticket to Boston. I've decided not to go after all."

"Boston's your home?"

"Yes. I mean, it was—"

"Home is where the heart is," the woman interrupted to agree wisely. "Now me, I'm goin' to Fort Worth to visit my sister."

"Fort Worth!" exclaimed the man who'd just stepped into line behind Meg. "I used to live in Fort Worth. Didn't like it much."

The conversation flowed around her as the line crept forward at a snail's pace. Meg shifted from foot to foot, wondering if she should just forget the refund and follow her heart. She and Jesse still had a lot of problems to iron out, but she'd be damned if she'd let him get away from her without knowing exactly how she felt. Yet each time she was on the verge of deciding to write off the ticket, the line would move just enough to keep her there.

"Where yawl goin'?"

It took Meg a moment to realize the question was directed at her by a nice-looking young man several places behind her in line.

"Boston," offered the talkative woman in front. "Home to Boston."

Meg smiled. "Well, actually—"

"I can't wait to hear this."

Jesse's harsh voice made the hair on the nape of her neck rise. Before she could respond, he caught her shoulder and spun her around. She found herself staring into his furious face, the most welcome sight in the world to her even with his brows lowered threateningly over eyes smoky with strong emotion.

"Jesse!" Her voice was a mere whisper.

His hands tightened on her shoulders. "You don't need a ticket."

"But—"

"Shut up and kiss me," he said.

His mouth crushed hers with a wild hunger that all but buckled her knees. She clung to him weakly, aware only of one wonderful thing as he raised his head and glowered down at her.

He had done the unthinkable. He had come after her.

He drew a great breath and set her away from him. "I needed that," he said. "Let's get out of here."

She shook her head; she couldn't find her voice.

Jesse leaned forward, his expression hard. "Don't even *think* about it," he advised in a voice that left no room for argument. "If you go to Boston, I'll just go after you. If you go to the ends of the earth, I'll find you."

She shook her head again, wanting to assure him that such drastic measures would not be necessary because she wasn't going anywhere. She was still too choked up to find words.

But he didn't understand. "Listen to me!" He spoke so fiercely that the shocked buzz of conversation around them faded away entirely. His attention on her never wavered. "I don't blame you for being mad, but I'm not going to let you run out on me again!"

She finally found her voice. "J-Jesse, I have to—"

"No, you don't! That's what I'm trying to tell you. I'm innocent. Look, just listen to what my *friend* has to say. That's all I ask."

Turning his head, Jesse indicated Joe Bob. Meg hadn't even realized he was there, so wrapped up was she in the powerful presence of her husband. Joe Bob had apparently been lurking in the background, no mean feat for a man his size.

Now he was front and center. Meg took one glance at him and gasped.

He looked as if he'd stepped into the path of a buzz saw. One puffy eye was black, one was red, and a scrape along his jaw might have been made by a fist. His cowboy shirt, several buttons shy, hung out of the waistband of his jeans, and his hat was crushed and shapeless.

The term "hangdog expression" might have been invented for Joe Bob Brooks.

Meg glanced from one man to the other without understanding. "Were you in an accident?" she asked at last, deciding nothing short of that could account for Joe Bob's condition.

The big man groaned. "Lordy, don't I wish! Way ol' J.J. drove gettin' here, it's a wonder. Never dreamed you could drive from Hell's Bells to San Antone in less than an hour."

He snatched off his hat and shook his head, hunching his shoulders defensively. He rolled the brim between awkward hands. "Ol' J.J. here cleaned my plow is all—not that I didn't deserve it," he added hastily, darting his companion a wary glance.

"You mean—" shocked, Meg turned on Jesse "—you two had a fight?"

"Oh, it was no fight," Joe Bob corrected quickly. "Fights we been havin' since we was still wet behind the ears. Nah, this was more like...divine retribution."

Jesse made an impatient growling noise deep in his chest. "Just tell her, Joe Bob. Cut the bull and tell her what happened."

"I'm a'fixin' to do that very thing," Joe Bob insisted. He gave her a sickly smile. "You see Meg, it's like this…" He looked down at his pointy-toed boots and swallowed hard. "I, uh, sorta played a little joke on my old pal J.J. here." He gave a feeble laugh. "Heh-heh-heh."

No one responded in kind. He gulped again and rolled his eyes. "Uhh…well, he come by real late that night, or I should say, real early the next mornin'—"

"What night?"

Jesse answered. "The night I got on my high horse and walked out on you. I found me an all-night diner and sat there drinking coffee and trying to figure out— well, trying to figure out *everything*. On the way back to the cabin, I stopped by Joe Bob's place."

"This is beginning to sound suspiciously like an explanation," Meg exclaimed. Joy filled her. Could the leopard change its spots, after all?

"Gonna rub my nose in it?" he shot back, eyes glittering. He turned his wrath on Joe Bob. "Tell the rest of it, cowboy, and talk fast."

"Oh, right, sure." Joe Bob's face fell. "Anything you say, J.J. Well, he come by and I'd had…company that night, so I just sorta slipped some stuff into his jacket pocket. Figured when he found it he'd get a good laugh. Heh-heh-heh?"

The lady in line ahead of Meg leaned forward. "What kinda stuff?" she asked in a shocked whisper. "Boy, this is better than that 'Dallas' TV show!"

Joe Bob bridled. "Do you mind?" he demanded. "This is a private powwow between friends."

The lady sniffed and lifted her chin high. "With friends like you, who needs enemies?"

"*Next,*" called the ticket clerk sternly, as if he'd said it several times already. With a final glance of condemnation for Joe Bob, the woman picked up her bag and marched to the counter.

"Say it all," Jesse ordered, his attention steady on Meg.

"Yeah, I'm gonna." Joe Bob shuffled his feet and wadded up his hat brim some more. "I been doin' his laundry all along, Meg—I mean, not me personal. But he's been bringin' it over to my place and throwin' it in with mine."

He took a deep breath, visibly bracing himself. "Lordy, Meg, I surely do owe you an apology," he burst out. "I don't reckon you'll ever forgive me. Hell, if the boot was on the other leg, I sure wouldn't. But I want you to know I am one sorry son of a—"

"Watch your language!"

"—gun! Right, J.J., you got it!" The big man gulped, his face reddening even more. "*I'm sorry,* Meg. I apologize—Lord, do I apologize! I'd like to convince you it was all a joke done in good fun . . . ?"

She shook her head slowly from side to side. It wasn't a joke in good fun and never had been. It was malice, pure and simple. Joe Bob wasn't eager to share his childhood friend's attentions with a wife, especially not some high-handed Yankee wife.

That stubborn Yankee wife had made it easy for him to undercut and manipulate her, but she wasn't dumb enough to fall for the "all-a-joke" defense. So what should she do about Joe Bob now?

"Next!"

At the ticket clerk's call, Meg saw a reprieve and started forward. Jesse caught her arm and tried to draw her away, but she resisted.

He frowned. "You don't have any business in this line," he said gruffly, as if trying to hide a growing doubt that she might.

"Yes, I do," she said with quiet force.

He actually flinched, and his face paled. "You mean, after all this, you still don't believe me?" He looked stunned. "Okay, in that case I guess I'll have to tell you everything."

"Lord have mercy!" Joe Bob moaned.

THEY STOOD in a tight little circle of three, speaking in low intense voices that occasionally rose above the babble around them as the line parted to flow past. Meg was aware of nothing except the willingness of the man she loved to talk to her about a subject that made him squirm with embarrassment.

"Yeah, I got lipstick on my collar that night from hell," Jesse conceded. "I'm comin' out of the arena after nearly gettin' my brains scrambled by fifteen hundred pounds of mean Brahma bull and some little rodeo groupie runs up and throws herself on top of me."

His lip curled and he made a sharp gesture with one hand. "She'd been hangin' around me ever since the rodeo started—hell, I don't know why. She didn't have any more sense than a june bug, but she sure as hell was persistent." He groaned. "You got any idea how hard it is to respect a woman who'll act like that?"

Joe Bob nodded sagely. "Yeah, boy, they're all over you. A cowboy don't stand a chance, I mean it." He seemed to realize what he'd said and added hastily, "That is, *regular* cowboys don't—ol' J.J. here is a special case. He never chased any a' them cute little—"

"Shut up, Joe Bob."

"Sure, J.J., sure."

"Go get a cup of coffee. Better yet, take the truck and go back to Hell's Bells." Jesse fished the keys from his pocket and tossed them into the air.

Joe Bob caught the keys on the fly. "But how'll you get...?" One glance at Jesse's thoroughly disgusted expression and Joe Bob threw up his hands in surrender. "None a' my business. I'm gone." Almost as an afterthought he added cautiously, "Nice talkin' to you, Meg." He looked at her hopefully.

"Joe Bob."

He stiffened when she said his name, his shoulders squaring as if he anticipated a blow.

"Look at me, Joe Bob."

Slowly he turned. Meg leaned forward and spoke with total sincerity. "You don't fool me for a minute, Joe Bob Brooks. I may not be a Texan, but I didn't just fall off the chowder wagon. I wouldn't want you to leave thinking I believe for a minute that baloney about it all being a big joke."

His face fell; his jowls practically quivered with disappointment. His gaze darted from her face to Jesse's, where he found no encouragement. "Yeah, well, thanks for sharing that." He sounded pathetic, not flippant.

"That said—" Meg heaved a sigh of resignation "—I'm willing to give it another go if you are."

"You mean...?" Hope sprang eternal.

"I mean I'm willing to let you go on living, but if you ever pull—or try to pull, or even mention—a practical joke in my presence I... I won't be responsible for what happens. In fact, it's too horrible to contemplate."

He looked as if in his excitement he might reach out and grab her in a bear hug; in self-defense, she stuck out her hand. "Is it a deal?"

"Oh, Lordy yes! Deal!" Joe Bob grabbed her hand and pumped it vigorously. "Meggie-gal, you may not be a Texan, but you are undoubtedly the best little ol'—"

"Don't push your luck," Jesse growled.

Joe Bob didn't; he galloped away without a backward glance, although a subdued "Yiiippee!" drifted back to them.

Jesse looked at Meg and licked his lips. "That was damned decent of you, Meggie, givin' him another chance. I admire that—that and the fact that you're not the kind of woman who'd run up to a strange man and try to kiss him."

His distaste was so obvious that for the first time she realized how much of a mystery aggressive women were to him. She, on the other hand, could understand if not sanction his attraction for them.

He honestly has no idea how special he is, she thought, *how handsome, how wonderful, how appealing.* Even if he did, it wouldn't make an ounce of difference to a man of his integrity.

He was still speaking. "I never understood this cowboy stuff. What the hell's a cowboy except a man dumb enough to chase cows and ride wild animals for a living? But all those women..." He shook his head as if in disbelief. "Even my wedding ring didn't discourage most of 'em."

He held out his left hand, manipulating his wedding band with his thumb. Automatically Meg touched the third finger of her left hand—and gasped.

She'd literally thrown her ring away! She raised stricken eyes to his.

Jesse took her hand and drew it forward. Reaching into his pocket, he pulled out her gold wedding band. Holding it poised before her finger, he lifted vulnerable eyes to hers.

"Say you believe me," he said in a thick voice.

"I believe you."

And she did. Looking at this man she loved, Meg understood at last that he was really hers, all hers. As he slipped the ring onto her finger, she knew she'd always believed in his basic goodness; she'd just fallen victim to the same stubbornness that infected him.

"You know," he said, looking down at her hand with the wedding ring in its rightful place, "I was wrong about a lot of things. When you left the last time, I knew you'd come back if I told you I'd been hurt. I didn't want you to know, because I didn't think I wanted you back under those circumstances."

She nodded, too filled with emotion to speak.

"I was wrong." He lifted his head suddenly, and she saw the depth of feeling in his eyes. "I want you back under any circumstances, any circumstances at all."

And then he said the words she most longed to hear. "I need you, Meggie. I don't ever want to live without you again."

He caught her around the waist, drew her close and kissed her.

She wrapped her arms around him and gave herself up to the magic once more. She was where she belonged, in the arms of the one man in all the world who could make her see fireworks every single time he touched her.

He lifted his head and she became aware on some dim level that they were the object of considerable approval from those still waiting in line, from beaming ticket clerks to smiling travelers hurrying past. She felt her cheeks burn, but this time it was as much with pride as embarrassment. She tipped her head back so she could see his face. "I love you," she said, "and I'm finally sure you love me, too."

He grinned. "You got that right!" He slid his hand down her arm and grasped her wrist. "Let's get out of here, darlin'."

"Next!" the airline clerk squawked.

"Wait a minute, wait a minute!" She cast a harried glance at the line and resisted the pull of his hand. "I've still got to—"

He dropped his arms to his sides and fell back a pace. He looked completely stunned; she'd seen that same expression on his face once when he'd been kicked in the solar plexus by a horse.

"If you love me, why are you still in this line?" he roared.

The few individuals within hearing range who *hadn't* been openly watching or more subtly eavesdropping immediately rectified their error. Meg ignored them and lifted her chin stubbornly.

Jesse groaned. *Not again,* his expression said.

Without another word, Meg marched up to the counter and slapped down her ticket. "I would like a refund on this ticket to Boston," she declared in ringing tones.

She turned, her laughing glance seeking Jesse as those in line behind her erupted with cheers and applause. Giving him her sexiest come-hither smile, she crooked her forefinger at him.

He stepped up beside her, moving like a man in deep shock. She touched his cheek with loving fingertips. "I had to get back in line to get my refund," she said gently. "I'm not going to Boston, I'm going with you."

Jesse let out a cowboy whoop, and picking her up, he whirled her around in a circle. She clung to his shoulders, laughing, deliriously happy.

He set her down just as the loudspeaker announced that Flight 333 to Boston was finally ready to board. The smiling clerk completed the transaction as Meg and Jesse simply stood there, looking into each other's eyes. The voice of the clerk pulled them back to reality. "I love a happy ending, but I've still got to say it—*next!*"

"Sorry, pardner. We'll get out of your way." Jesse grabbed Meg's hand and pulled her after him toward the exit. She had to skip to keep up, hanging on to his hand for dear life—for he was her dear life.

"You gave Joe Bob the truck," she gasped. "How will we get back to the cabin?"

"We won't. Not until tomorrow, anyway, and we'll worry about that when the time comes."

"But..." Meg zigzagged to avoid a toddler who stumbled into her path. She cast an anxious glance behind her, relieved to see the child scooped up out of harm's way by his mother.

Jesse squeezed her hand. "Don't argue," he commanded, although arguing was the furthest thing from her mind. "We'll grab a cab to the Menger."

"What's a Menger?"

He stopped abruptly and swung her around to face him. He caught her other hand and his smile grew even broader. She thought she'd never seen him look so happy.

"A hotel in San Antonio. That's my idea of heaven," he drawled. "A night in a hotel overlooking the Alamo, with you providin' the fireworks."

She matched his drawl. "You sure got *that* right."

And as it turned out, he did.

THEY CALLED RANDY from their hotel room early the next morning. Meg had bargained for the right to tell their son the good news, but with the moment at hand, she found herself too choked with emotion to say the words.

"Your father has something to tell you," she finally blurted, and handed the telephone to Jesse.

Walking to the window, she pushed aside the draperies and looked down at the Alamo Plaza. The old mission gleamed in pale splendor in the strong sunlight, a visible symbol of the indomitable spirit of Texas. The same indomitable spirit burned in Jesse and made him the man he was—stubborn, proud, honorable.

"That's right," she heard him say. "Uh-huh, we miss you, too...that's right, we'll all be together soon." He glanced at Meg and smiled his slow sexy smile. "A couple days, anyway. Your mother and I have...some things to take care of first."

He winked at her and she felt the blush warming every part of her. This time, however, it was a blush of understanding.

He was still talking to Randy. "Sorry, kid, but you'll just have to be patient a little longer. Trust me. It'll be worth it when we're all together again as a family." He listened for a few moments with a smile on his face, muttered, "Yep!" and hung up.

"So what did he say?" Meg crossed the room to slide her arms around her husband's waist. She pressed her cheek against the smooth brown skin of his chest and sighed contentedly.

Jesse enveloped her in his arms and hugged her tight. "He said, 'You got that right, Dad!'"

Meg laughed. "You do, you know."

"Yes." He pulled back enough to see her face. "Meg, there's one more thing I have to say to you—that I have to be sure you understand."

She groaned and closed her eyes. "Now what?"

"I didn't let Thom T. blackmail me into this crazy scheme because of Randy. That's what you thought, right? That I only came because of Randy?"

"Well, yes...." It hurt to admit it.

He shook his head. "That wasn't the reason. I could have fought you for custody if I was only interested in Randy."

"You...you considered going for custody?" The words made her throat ache.

"Not really. I *thought* about it, I didn't consider it. You know what I realized?"

She shook her head.

"I realized that I came here for you—for us." He took a deep breath. "I love the son we made together, but first of all I love you. Thom T. could have held a gun to my head and it wouldn't have mattered otherwise. I think that's why you came, too—because you love me, always did and always will." He gave her a wary glance. "So what do you think about that, Margaret Randall Taggart?"

"In the immortal words of my son and my husband—" Meg rose on tiptoe "—you got that right!" And she wrapped her arms around his neck and kissed him until he hollered uncle—which took the rest of that day and part of the next.

* * * * *

Jesse's brother will soon have a stormy reunion of his own in SHOWDOWN! Daniel Boone Taggart doesn't know it yet, but he's about to return to Texas—and to Kit McCrae. Harlequin Romance #3242
The Bridal Collection
Available in January 1993
wherever paperbacks are sold

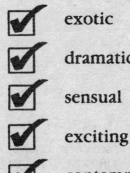

WELCOME TO

The quintessential small town where everyone knows everybody else!

Finally, books that capture the pleasure of tuning in to your favorite TV show!

GREAT READING... GREAT SAVINGS... AND A FABULOUS FREE GIFT!

Each book set in Tyler is a self-contained love story; together, the twelve novels stitch the fabric of the community. The covers honor the old American tradition of quilting; each cover depicts a patch of the large Tyler quilt.

With Tyler you can receive a fabulous gift ABSOLUTELY FREE by collecting proofs-of-purchase found in each Tyler book. And use our special Tyler coupons to save on your next TYLER book purchase.

Join your friends at Tyler for the sixth book, SUNSHINE by Pat Warren, available in August.

When Janice Eber becomes a widow, does her husband's friend David provide more than just friendship?